HOUSES DIVIDED

Houses of the Dead: Book One

LEAH R CUTTER

Knotted Road Press

Houses Divided
Houses of the Dead: Book One
Copyright © 2020 Leah Cutter
All rights reserved
Published by Knotted Road Press
www.KnottedRoadPress.com

ISBN: 978-1-64470-187-4

Cover Art:

ID 36107750 © Dusan Kostic | Dreamstime.com

Cover and interior design copyright © 2020 Knotted Road Press
http://www.KnottedRoadPress.com

Reviews

It's true. Reviews help me sell more books. If you've enjoyed this story, please consider leaving a review of it on your favorite site.

Come someplace new…

Are you a traveler? Do you enjoy exploring strange new worlds, new cultures, new people?

Journey into the various lands envisioned by Leah Cutter.

Sign up for my newsletter and I'll start you on your travels with a free copy of my book, *The Island Sampler*.

http://www.LeahCutter.com/newsletter/

Also by Leah R Cutter

Forgotten Gods

A Wind Blown Torment

A Stone Strewn Clash

A Sea Washed Victory

Tanish Empire Trilogy

The Glass Magician

The Desert Heart

The Ghost Dog

The Cassie Stories

Poisoned Pearls

Tainted Waters

Spoiled Harvest

Bloodied Ice

The Witch's Progress

Circle of Air

Circle of Water

Circle of Fire

Circle of Earth

Seattle Trolls

The Changeling Troll

The Princess Troll

The Fairy-Bridge Troll

The Troll-Demon War

The Troll-Human War

The Troll-Troll War

The Shadow Wars Trilogy

The Raven and the Dancing Tiger

The Guardian Hound

War Among the Crocodiles

The Clockwork Fairy Kingdom

The Clockwork Fairy Kingdom

The Maker, the Teacher, and the Monster

The Dwarven Wars

The Chronicles of Franklin

Franklin Versus The Popcorn Thief

Franklin Versus The Soul Thief

Franklin Versus The Child Thief

Huli Intergalactic - Science/Space Fantasy

Origins

The Strawberry Girl

Contemporary Fantasy

Siren's Call

The Immortals' War

Chapter One

HOUSE OF CRYSTAL

HAPTOMI HELD himself rigid as he carefully walked down the narrow stone stairs. It simply wouldn't do for him to brush up against the roughly hewn rock wall on his left and possibly stain his pristine white and yellow robes with the slime and mold that always accumulated there. To his right, nothing protected him from the utter darkness of the vast chamber, as well as the potentially deadly fall down two stories onto the sharp rocks below.

The light from the top of the stairs grew thinner as he descended. That was the best way he could think to describe it. The darkness below ate away at the brightness, consumed the streams of gold from the candles, until the light abruptly vanished as he stepped off the stairs and onto the earth itself.

Haptomi took a deep breath, the staleness of the air almost comforting. He had taken this path so many times before, once every ten days for over thirty years. Though he had turned fifty, he still had at least a decade left as the head of the Temple of Truth, the Goddess Morta willing to let his soul remain and the God Djediese continuing to grant him magic.

I

Eyes shut, hands by his side, Haptomi stretched out his fingers, imagining long tendrils of golden light flowing from the tips down into the ground itself, waking his landsense.

There it was. A vast flow of awareness surged up and spread out. Haptomi knew exactly where he stood, both in terms of how far under the earth he was as well as his location in terms of other natural features, such as the mountains, the forests, and the rivers.

It wasn't necessarily a comfortable feeling. Every time he pushed his senses into the earth, he felt as though it pushed back, not wanting to be disturbed, particularly not by the ants who crawled through it, the beings so puny compared to itself.

Haptomi hummed a hymn of soothing thanks that the earth recognized him, that he could still detect its greatness and glory.

Eventually, Haptomi knew that the gift of the God Djediese would weaken and disappear, his landsense failing him. He would be left alone to struggle in the darkness. Few people retained their sense of the land after they turned seventy. Many passed away at that point, falling prey to a wasting disease referred to as the Abandonment.

How long before Haptomi would lose his landsense? How many years did he actually have left?

That was a question for the dead, not that Haptomi would bother asking any of them.

Having found his spot in the earth, Haptomi sent his landsense out through the utter darkness, seeking what was before him.

A spark of jagged rock pricked his consciousness. Haptomi bravely made his way forward, toward it. He kept his eyes closed, relying on his magical senses to guide him.

Several yards ahead of him lay the Chamber of Crystals. He remembered the first time he'd felt it, how cold and brittle the living crystals seemed him, lying there in the heart of the overwhelming darkness. How sluggishly the crystals danced, captured by the shattered rock.

As always, Haptomi tried to judge the strength of his sense of the chamber ahead. It seemed no weaker or stronger than usual. His landsense wasn't fading yet.

There were stories of the dead rising up to guide a priest to their destination, or sometimes to vex them. Haptomi doubted that he would rate such consideration. He lived at a time of great peace—five years now that the four lands had been ruled jointly by four great houses. Before, there had been constant border wars and between the houses.

Light shining against Haptomi's shut eyes made him open them. He relaxed slightly when he saw that he wasn't imagining the light. No, the crystals in the chamber up ahead *had* started to glow. He hadn't been imagining his sense of the chamber—another of his greatest fears. He had been walking directly toward it, not stumbling around in the dark like a disgraceful drunkard.

White and yellow light pierced the darkness, sliding out of the opening and trickling across his path. The colors changed as he drew closer, shades of red and blue interrupting the brilliance, darkening the hues. Waves of light chased each other across the walls as the chamber awoke. It reminded Haptomi of the dances warriors did to warm up every morning, slowly pushing their hands through the air from one side to the other.

While a very popular poem referred to the Chamber of Crystals as "spilling its golden light out into the world," Haptomi never saw the light as golden. There were too many individual colors to give it a solid whole. It was more like a living rainbow, the same which cloaked the God Djediese, who directed the Temple of Truth.

The entrance to the chamber was perfectly round and at

least ten feet tall, as if a giant had struck the earth with a tremendously large hammer. No one remembered how the entrance had been found, who had carved the stone steps leading to the underground chamber, or how the crystals had been taught to speak.

Everyone knew the consequences of taking even a single rock from the chamber, how the lights would flee and bad luck would stalk all four of the lands until the thief was found and the crystal returned.

Haptomi stepped just inside the chamber and stopped. The chamber was round, like the inside of a beautiful geode that had been expertly cracked open, several yards in diameter. Rough crystals stuck out from all sides, sharp spikes that easily sliced through skin. While some of the crystals were as fat and stubby as his thumbs, others were huge, easily the size of a small child.

It was like stepping into a completely foreign landscape. Nothing manmade was tolerated by the chamber. The crystals blazed in all their glory, streams of red, blue, and now, yes, some golden light undulating like ribbons in the wind, flowing across the walls.

Haptomi closed his eyes and focused on his task so he would not be mesmerized by the dancing light. More than one myth told of priests and priestesses turned to crystal by the lights, having stayed too long in the chamber.

Privately, Haptomi doubted that was possible. While the lights were fascinating, it didn't take that much to break their hold.

Or maybe he was just more practical than most.

Haptomi pushed out with his senses again, used his landsense to judge the readiness of the chamber, hoping that the crystals were willing to reply to a question. Though he visited every tenth day, he could never say for certain if the chamber would answer or not. The longest "rest" it had ever taken had been nearly ninety days, though that hadn't happened in his lifetime. During the height of the last great war, though questions were asked almost daily, the chamber generally only responded once every ten to fifteen days.

All questions had to be framed correctly. The crystals responded solely with names, and only of those people with strong landsense who had spent at least a year in the city of Nyati which sprawled above the chamber. General questions like, "Who will win the war?" brought resounding silence and abrupt darkness.

When the feeling of spikiness faded to a background murmur that others had compared to the sound of far-away ocean waves, Haptomi finally sung his question.

Which person shall attend the next court of the ghosts?

The question was an important one, inquiring who should spend a year seeing to the needs of the ghosts and their court. Frequently, those who were chosen went on to either become the LandHolder, or they became the Holder for an important household. Though the House of Crystal shouldn't need a new LandHolder for at least two decades, as the duties had only recently been passed along to Ibitsima, it was still of vital interest who might be the next, which of her three children would be favored.

Haptomi drew a sigh of relief when a warming hum came in response. It meant that the chamber had accepted his question and would answer it.

The humming noise increased, until a bright chorale of notes began, rising and falling. The sound was impossible to replicate. Was that because the music was in the head of the person standing inside the chamber? Were there actually no sounds being played that anyone else could hear? No sound was ever heard outside of the chamber, even when the crystals could be coaxed to speak in front of an audience.

It was strange. Even the dead made noise, albeit of a quiet sort.

Haptomi felt his heart stir with the quick notes. It surprised him how worked up the crystals appeared to be that morning. Was there actually something to this seemingly innocent question? Some sort of great change being heralded?

The sound faded quickly, as if consensus was just a matter of a few arguments—that everyone saw the necessity of the accord but had to grumble about it first.

A name came floating through the space, as clearly as if sung by a single throat.

Akalina.

That…was an interesting choice.

The girl was, what, fourteen years old, if he was remembering correctly. He had been certain that the chamber would have named an adult. If it was to be a younger person, it should have been one of the three children of Ibitsima, or even a direct relation of hers. That would have been more expected.

Instead, it had named someone from a different line. Still connected, but it was tenuous. She was the current LandHolder's sister's husband's brother's child—a cousin, but not a close one. If you looked at heirs as concentric circles, the current LandHolder's three children would belong in the first circle, her sister's children would be in the second circle, while Akalina was definitely part of the third circle.

He'd never really thought about the girl. Couldn't recall her, not exactly. All he had was an impression of a dark cloud, with wispy black hair and a pale face.

Any child who spent a year attending the ghost court was eligible to become the next LandHolder. The land itself would choose, of course, when it came time.

Maybe next year one of the LandHolder's own children would be selected by the Chamber of Crystals.

In the meantime, there was nothing Haptomi could do about the ruling. No clarifying questions he could ask. The chamber had spoken.

There was more than one myth of an official messenger who didn't actually listen to the crystals, who then proclaimed his or her own choice instead, a selection that would be the most advantageous for the Temple of Truth.

However, all of those myths also emphasized the consequences that occurred when a priest or priestess was tempted that way: Crops that withered despite the rain; plagues of locusts or hordes of birds that stripped fields clean; children turned into ghosts before the eyes of their parents.

Haptomi sang his thanks to the chamber and to the crystals for their wisdom. His words fell flat. Frequently the chamber would sing back, carrying the tune and softly changing it, echoing and refracting the melody until it faded away.

Today, silence greeted him. Even before he'd turned away, the lights started fading.

Was it his landsense that was finally failing him?

Or was the news he carried bigger than the little girl herself?

Chapter Two
HOUSE OF COBALT

AUGURY WAS ALWAYS TRICKY.

Belam fussed with the placement of his braziers again, shifting the black cast-iron pots just a hair this way and that, making sure that the four aligned perfectly with the cardinal points of the compass he felt deep inside his bones.

Outside of the primary four braziers, each precisely one foot away, he had placed a secondary set of four braziers, each midway between the others. He'd instructed workers to carve deep grooves in the stone running between the pots, both the major and the minor. That morning, he'd carefully strewn ground charcoal into the runnels, the faintest smell of burned wood still lingering.

Solid rock surrounded Belam. If he reached his hands up above his head, his fingertips would scrape against the rough rock. Smokeless torches lined the walls, glowing with phosphorous stone instead of fire. The pale light gave harsh outlines to the braziers, casting multiple shadows across the hard rock floor. Stale air filled the manmade cave, as no natural winds could ever cleanse this place, even when the door was open.

A doorway had been carved in the northern wall, opposite where Belam would cast his augury. The wooden door was shut tightly against the outside world, felted fabric stuffed into all the cracks so that no air could escape, no errant breezes could disturb the sacred smoke.

All four houses had Temples of Truth that used their own methods for peering into the future. The House of Crystal had their crystal chamber. The House of Pearl had deep, natural caves along the coast, where tidal pools would turn to silver, like the best mirrors, and would reflect the world to come. The House of Gold threw braids of wheat across cloths covered in letters, the placement of the strands indicating answers to their questions.

Only the House of Cobalt dealt with smoke and the dead directly. While the others might think that their prettified auguries gave them insight from the gods, those from the House of Cobalt knew that their answers came from the dead, the ones who lived beyond the veils of the world and were strong enough to reach through time to direct the living. They were the blessed of the Goddess Morta, she who birthed the world as well as brought death. The God Djediese, who directed the Temple of Truth, gave the people the magic to be able to talk to the dead and receive the messages from the gods.

The messages all came from beyond the grave, though.

Belam checked the placement of his braziers one last time before he took his spot at the southernmost tip, the place of power on which everything else rested. He removed his long leather apron and placed it carefully to the side. It had done its job, protecting the intricately embroidered shirt underneath, that had been handed down to him from the former head priestess of the Temple of Truth when Belam had stepped into her role. Though the shirt was primarily cobalt blue, it had narrow stripes of black, white, and gold between the bands of geometric patterns. Beneath that, Belam wore fine linen trousers, the color of polished nickel, and black boots similar to those that miners wore.

Slowly, Belam tied a wet kerchief over his nose and mouth. It had been soaked in lavender water. He felt drops of water splash down on his shirt and frowned with dismay.

Hopefully the drops weren't noticeable and he would still appear presentable. As the head priest of the Temple of Truth, he did have appearances to maintain. Even with the dead.

With a snap of his fingers, Belam used his magic to light all the braziers at the same time. Each held a mixture of incense, charcoal, and yes, cobalt. It was dangerous to use the most sacred of elements in an augury, though it was also the most powerful element.

Smelting cobalt at high enough temperatures produced a deadly gas. Though Belam wasn't intending on running his augury fires that hot, it was always a risk. Lesser priests had been known to die from distraction and the smoke that resulted.

Belam called out the names of his ancestors, as well as previous LandHolders and heroes of old. They would stand as his guardians when he opened the portal to the underworld. He felt them gather around him, could almost hear them greedily sucking in the precious smoke the braziers generated.

Despite the wet cloth, Belam soon found it difficult to breathe. It was yet another risk of those who followed the traditional forms for performing augury, the possibility of sucking in too much smoke and becoming overwhelmed by it.

Belam only recited about half of the list of guardian names that he'd originally memorized. It would take too much time to call all of them. And really, how much protection did he need? They would only be called on if his other defenses failed.

When Belam finished calling his guardians and the regular part of the augury, smoke bellowed out of the braziers as usual. However, this time, it was as if bellows had been placed beneath them, venting large amounts of smoke. Man-like shapes began to form in the clouds.

He knew that he could ask simple questions of these souls, such as who in the court should be betrothed to the youngest of the LandHolder's children.

Today's question was much more important.

Belam impatiently threw out lines of protective fire that raced along the grooves the workers had chiseled out. The blue and green magical flames shot up high, strong enough to guard him from whoever might rush through the portal he was opening, rising up from the underworld and desperate for a chance among the living.

The Goddess Morta had set her warriors—also known as demons—to live in the underworld. Those who obeyed her merely tested the souls of those passing through, giving the newly dead the experience they needed to be worthy of passing over the oceans of light to the Golden Lands.

The demons who did not obey the goddess built their own armies of followers, not allowing souls to pass along.

After much research, Belam had come to the conclusion that the demons were closer to the gods than the ghosts. And it was the demons who Belam intended to question that morning. He'd read the ancient texts provided by the merchant Benitoyo, knew that it was possible to call on the demons and make them do his bidding.

The smell of sulfur blew over Belam. His skin tingled from the intense heat. Sweat poured down his back. He drew the lines of protective fire up higher along the inner square, so that the flames licked the ceiling. The rock there blackened, which was unusual for magical fires. A loud crack shot through the air, the stone along the floor that held the channels cracking from the intense heat.

Though the Temple of Truth had used this room for augury for years, it might now be spoiled, unable to be properly cleansed.

No matter. Belam could always order his minions to carve him out a new one.

He tried to rein the fires in, both in his braziers and along the floor, but they fought him. Winds from the underworld fed the flames now. He didn't have much time, not given the bellowing smoke.

Belam rushed through the incantation to open the portal door, taking short breaths through his mouth. He needed to ask his question before time ran out. He felt dizzy and the tips of his fingers tingled from the lack of air. Hopefully he wouldn't ruin his fine shirt, though it was going to need a serious cleaning.

A black void appeared in the center of the square, like a hole carved out of daylight and filled with nightmares. It was considerably larger than Belam had expected, man-sized instead of merely the size and shape of a man's head.

Still, Belam pushed on. He called on those who had long since passed but who had stayed in the underworld, those known demons who still worked *with* the Goddess Morta. He begged them for their presence now in the land of the living, to carry their wisdom to him.

Dark smoke trembled around the edges of the cavity in the center of his square, shivering as if it had been drawn from the warmth out into the cold.

Belam's eyes watered fiercely. He couldn't rely on what he was seeing. Did ghosts carved out of the blackness stand there before him? Shapes he could barely make out?

"Oh hear my plea!" Belam cried out. "Tell me, who is to be the next LandHolder?"

It was a question that a regular augury could not answer, not by those beings who spent most of their time sharing the world of the living. Or, as Belam had long suspected, would not answer, whether they knew the truth or not.

But he *had* to know. The Temple of Truth deserved an answer. Kinaki, their current LandHolder, lay on his deathbed. The temple had to know whether the next LandHolder was Chaotu, the eldest son who didn't care much for Belam and the other priests, or Lijun, the daughter. She was strong-headed, but at the same time, adored the temple and had talked about becoming a priestess herself. The Temple needed to prepare for either outcome.

The question was considered unorthodox by many. Some old fuddy-duddies might even consider it inappropriate.

That was in part why Belam had had to call on darker forces, to speak with those from the underworld, to compel them to tell him the truth.

An echo of a scream sliced the air behind him.

What in the name of the Great Granite Tombs was that?

It sounded for all the world like a ghost dying. Though that didn't make any sense. Weren't ghosts already dead?

Belam turned his head, just for a moment, to look to the side.

He realized his mistake immediately.

The instant he took his attention away from his augury square, darkness poured out from the portal. It had been waiting for him to release it all along, biding its time.

Black figures snuffed out his walls of protective fire, howling and dying as they did so. More came, piling on top of the fallen bodies.

The comforting ghosts surrounding Belam died valiantly, snuffed out by the horrible figures pouring through the portal, creatures from nightmares come to live and breed in the land of the living.

None of them touched Belam. Instead, they blew foul smelling smoke at him, overwhelming him, stealing what little of his breath remained.

Coughing, Belam fell hard on his knees. The pain brought him to his senses for a moment. Blinking away the tears, he thought he saw a dark figure dancing with one of red-tinted ghosts. No, not dancing. Fighting.

The colors of each were bleeding into the other, the blackness now highlighted with a red glow, while the heart of the whiter ghost was now filled with the blackest night.

Belam swayed where he knelt, trying to get back on his feet. He *had* to close the portal before more creatures of nightmare snuck into the world of the living. Before all the ghosts of the House of Cobalt were infected with demons from the underworld.

One of the dark creatures saw him trying to rise up and deliberately send a wave of vomitous smoke in Belam's direction. He fell to the ground, coughing, trying to clear his lungs of the stench.

Did he just imagine that the creature he faced finally answered his question? Or was the whispered reply, "We shall take Kinaki's place," merely his own fears speaking?

The last sight Belam had before dying was the wooden door being ripped off its hinges and the light that poured into the chamber suckling the darkness born there.

Chapter Three

HOUSE OF GOLD

TORJA SIGHED as she looked at how her fletche had scattered across her telling cloth. The fletche were made from dried wheat stalks, braided in a complicated pattern. Each piece was not much longer than her palm, the ends tied with bright red string. The telling cloth was her best one, brilliant white with hand-painted golden letters. She sat outside the Temple of Truth in a back garden despite the cold winds and the threatening rain clouds. Brown shot through the grass, old grass having died that winter. Though it was only the second month of the new year, she could already see the nubs of new shoots pushing through the rich earth, the spring reclaiming the land.

While it was important to include every letter in their alphabet on the telling cloth, the placement of the letters was a personal choice. As part of the training of every priestess and priest of the Temple of Truth, the novice would spend time meditating on the importance of each letter, as well as the words starting with that letter. Before moving on to the next letter, they would paint that letter onto their first telling cloth, in the place or position that spoke personally to them.

There were tales, of course, of the slow learner who spent his lifetime coming up with the placement of each letter and who only cast a single augury before he died, though it was a very important and accurate augury. Or the priestess who rushed through her letters and ended up foretelling an inaccurate doom every time she threw the fletche.

That afternoon, it appeared that the future didn't want to be read. Most of Torja's fletche had landed at the edges of her telling cloth. None rested in the center. It couldn't have been the wind. It wasn't that strong, despite the rainclouds overhead. Plus, she'd had the same difficulty doing an augury inside the temple earlier.

While there were important letters along the border of the cloth, the way the fletche had jumbled up along the edges of it made it impossible to determine their alignment. More than one had fallen together on letters. Normally, when a fletche fell, the direction of the piece gave a hint to the other letters in the word, or even words, of the augury.

Torja shivered in her warm green wool coat. She reached out to pick up the fallen fletche, using her other hand to hold up the long opening of the sleeve.

The jacket she wore was cut in the traditional manner, with long sleeves opening up into huge cuffs that made it incredibly impractical when it came to actually doing anything. Her mentors had used the long sleeves to good advantage, waving an arm across the telling cloth and sweeping all the fletche to the side. She knew others who'd figured out how to store things in those huge sleeves.

Torja was just as likely to forget and leave her hands at her sides and have everything that she'd carried in them drop to the ground.

At least it was a pretty color, dark green, with beautiful black embroidery down the front and around the huge cuffs.

It went well with her pale, pinkish skin, long braided brunette hair, and soft green eyes.

She pushed herself up to grab at the fletche that landed at the far side of the telling cloth, then sat herself back down with a heavy sigh.

Should she try again? As the head priestess of the Temple of Truth, she shouldn't be having this much difficulty with a simple augury. She'd prayed regularly to the God Djediese, but he didn't seem inclined to listen to her. She'd even tried praying to the other gods as well, the Goddess Orolorg, who tended the fields and the fertility of the land, the God Xiuma who the merchants and miners all prayed to, who'd delighted in secreting beautiful gems and stones under the earth, treasures for others to find, making the land beneath the earth a beautiful place, even the Goddess Morta, mother of all, she who both brought the storms and calmed them.

All the gods ignored Torja's pleas, despite the fact that she was the head of the Temple of Truth.

Then again, no one had been more surprised than she when she'd been selected for the position. Sure, she'd been training for years beside her cohorts. But the two other primary candidates were more graceful and talented than she was. They'd also been born to important Holds. Particularly Ragna, who could trace her ancestry to one of the former LandHolder families. Torja was barely thirty, while the others were now in their forties.

Except, if Torja was honest with herself, the other acolytes didn't get along well with anyone but themselves and others in their temple. Torja, since she'd been at the bottom of the pecking order, had been the one sent off with messages to the other temples, to talk with the merchants' or miners' Holds, to speak with the various farmer or shepherd groups. Of course, she'd never talked with the nobles, her rivals had reserved those meetings for themselves.

It also meant that Torja gained a lot of experience doing auguries for individuals, not just for dignitaries.

Today's augury was supposed to be easy, asking about the spring harvest festival and which families should lead the procession.

She'd tried doing the augury inside the temple. But instead of spreading out, the fletche landed in an unreadable clump in the middle of her telling cloth.

So she thought she'd try it outside. See if the natural winds could help, but they'd scattered the fletche everywhere.

Should she try again? She looked down at the fletche in her hands. Counted.

There should have been ten. That was the traditional number, though there were methods for using as few as three or as many as twenty.

But she only held nine pieces.

Damn it! Where was the other one? She stuffed the fletche into their satchel, then scanned the ground, searching for the errant one.

She didn't see it anywhere.

With a sigh, she carefully looked down both her sleeves, seeing if it had gotten trapped up there.

Nope. Nothing but the woolen sleeve of her sweater, and under that, bare skin.

Torja pushed herself up to standing, stretching her hands far above her head, then bending at the waist and stretching out her back.

She spent far too much time sitting now, as head priestess, instead of walking everywhere in the city. Maybe she could insist that some of her meetings be held without chairs, as Unnir, the LandHolder, held her court.

She couldn't help the giggle that escaped at the thought of making MerchantHolder Justel, the fat and lazy head of the merchants' Hold, stand for an hour or more.

Though that may lead to shorter meetings and fewer arguments…

She sighed and shook her head at herself. There were only so many things that she could change, so many traditions that she could push at. She needed to maintain her position in the temple as well as in the court and not do anything that would appear to leave the temple weak.

A weak Temple of Truth, even during a time of peace, could be disastrous for everyone.

Torja stayed bent over as she had been, searching the ground for the missing fletche. Had the wind just picked it up and flung it away? She hadn't felt a strong breeze. But that didn't mean it hadn't happened.

She picked up the telling cloth and folded it into the traditional thirds. She still remembered the chastisement she'd received her very first year as a novice, when she'd dared to fold the cloth in quarters.

It was how she'd folded the linens for her mother when her mother's hands had grown weak and crippled with arthritis. It had been luck that her uncle had been able to pay for Torja to go into the temple when her mother had fallen ill.

Torja still missed her, though her mother had died many years before. While Torja knew it was selfish, she hoped that her mother had lingered in the underworld, and so kept track of her daughter's accomplishments before she'd traveled across the oceans of light to the Golden Lands.

After Torja properly folded her cloth and put it into the satchel with the *fletche*, she spent a few more moments looking for the missing one.

Wait, was it over there?

Torja took a moment to note her location. According to her landsense, she sat at due east, the most important of the cardinal points as that was where the sun, and hence all life, came from. The fletche had traveled far past where the edges of the cloth had been, and now pointed due south.

Was that something of importance? A significant occurrence? Or was it just random chance?

"Come here, you," Torja said, walking the two feet over to where the bright fletche lay against the brown and green grass.

Only when she lifted the small braid did she realize that it had been stuck to the back of a slug. The part of the fletche that faced downward was now covered in gray slime.

Ewww.

Had the fletche originally landed just off the edge of the cloth, and had the slug made off with it? She couldn't help but grin at the thought of a bandit slug, maybe with an eye patch and a tiny sword tied to its waist, stealing everything that he could lay his hands on.

Except that slugs didn't travel that quickly. No, it must have accidentally struck the slug when she'd first tossed the fletche into the air.

"My apologies, SlugHolder," Torja said. "I hope I have not inconvenienced you and your busy day."

The slug didn't respond but continued to slowly ooze away.

Torja wiped the fletche clean with her fingers, remembering only at the last moment not to then rub her hand clean against her coat. Instead, she reached down and wiped it across the grass. Though no one would say anything to her about cleaning her clothes, she still didn't like to make more work for others.

As Torja walked across the garden and back toward the Temple of Truth, she had to wonder why it had been so difficult to use augury for even the smallest of things the last few days.

And what that actually foretold.

Chapter Four
HOUSE OF PEARL

SHIMOKORO KNEW HE WAS EARLY. He paced the small strip of land at the back of the cave, the tide creeping in and cutting off his escape.

He could have come later. No one would think anything of it if he waded through the telling waters only moments before the time for augury drew to its fullest.

However, he didn't like disturbing the waters before an augury. That seemed gauche to him, disrespectful. It was why he wouldn't leave the cave immediately after the vision was presented to him, but instead, wait the many hours necessary until the tide had crept back out and he could leave with his feet dry.

There were tales of those who stepped into the waters before the vision was complete and therefore misinterpreted what was being shown to them. Shimokoro would never make that mistake. He had the patience and the discipline to see everything through to its logical conclusion.

He knew the value of waiting. Of planning. Of being part of the creation of something so much bigger than himself that only his heirs, or perhaps their heirs, would enjoy the full fruits of it.

Night crept across the land outside the cave. Shimokoro felt, rather than saw, the deepening of the dark and the rising of the moon. He'd already set dazzling lights against the rough rock walls of the cave, their luminescence silver and cold. The air smelled of the ocean, of salt and fish and seaweed. His stomach rumbled: as part of his preparation, his last meal of rich fish stew with onions had been several hours ago.

At least the cave was tall enough that he didn't have to duck his head. While most of the people from the House of Pearl tended to be short, Shimokoro was as tall as someone from the House of Gold, nearly six feet. He stood a head above most of his cohorts. His coloring was as dark as theirs, with kinky black hair and large black eyes. Even the skin of his palms was brown and not pink.

He wore his warmest robes made out of black felted wool, decorated with gold and silver thread, then studded not just with white pearls but also with precious black ones. Old fashioned attendants to the Temple of Truth wore sandals woven from straw, but Shimokoro wore boots to keep his feet warm and dry.

He was the head of the temple, and he could afford to have some comfort. Particularly with a seeing as important as this. He was certain that the God Djediese would send his attendants to talk with Shimokoro, to peel back the veils between now and the past.

The pool he walked next to was the largest of those maintained by the Temple of Truth. It was at least seven feet long and ten feet wide. It was also the furthest away from the temple and the capital city of Yawatan, two days' journey to the north.

The path to the cave had been carved out of sharp, black

obsidian, thrown there from a volcano less than a century in the past. White grasses grew out of the cervices. Lonely winds blew across the point of rock that grew out of the land into the waters. The constant sound of the surf echoed deeply in the cave, a booming noise that more than one poet had likened to the heartbeat of the land.

Shimokoro had a different sort of beauty in his heart. While others at the temple focused on painting or making pretty words, he maintained his warrior training. Every morning, Shimokoro spent time in the courtyard with the warriors, going through the warmup stretches he'd learned as a child. Now, in the cave, he pushed his hands slowly from one side to the other, imagining the air had turned viscous as bread dough, that he was surrounded by it and had to push his way through.

He paused his pacing, then fell into the first position of his warmup. He let his hands rise and fall slowly, like a gentle wave coming to shore. The breathing helped calm him. He chose the longer version of the warmup, where the center section was repeated, once to the right, then to the left.

When he finished, he closed his eyes for a few moments, just to breathe. The soft air of the cave caressed his cheeks. The smell of the sea filled and sustained him. It was only when he was perfectly still that he realized he could hear the quiet lapping of the pool at his feet, beyond the deep heartbeat of the waves.

Opening his eyes, Shimokoro realized that the time for augury had come.

First, Shimokoro thanked his ancestors for giving his family strength and the leaders of the House of Pearl wisdom. He thanked his predecessor at the Temple of Truth for having chosen him for this great task. And he thanked the lands, the waters, and the gods for sustaining him.

It didn't take much magic to light the still pool at his

feet. The silvery sheen pleased him enough that he smiled, though he returned to a more serious expression moments later.

Now was not the time for frivolity.

As the color of the waters grew more radiant, rainbows gathered in the far corners, as if invisible spray was being thrown up by the smooth surface. The lights appeared to chase each other, soft colors that lessened the purity of the silver.

Shimokoro frowned. He never trusted the dancing lights. They were a distraction. It wouldn't do for an augury to start and for him to be distracted by rainbows.

He focused on the center of the silvery pond instead, finally throwing out his question.

Is it time?

The churning of the waters surprised him. The smooth silver surface bubbled as as if a creature were rising from below.

He had no sword with which to defend himself, no shield to ward off another's blows. He still found himself automatically taking a crouching pose, ready to throw off an attacker.

Maybe he would end up getting his robes and boots wet after all.

But nothing sprang out of the waters. No monster from the deep flung itself at him.

The waters smoothed out suddenly, as if ropes of seaweed had dragged back down whatever had been below. Instead, a clear picture was shown to Shimokoro, as if he were actually standing in the room with Belam, his counterpart in the Temple of Truth for the House of Cobalt.

Shimokoro shivered as the great heat from Belam's fires poured out of the image.

He shivered again at the dark portal that Belam opened, the nightmarish creatures that it vomited out.

The vision died as Belam did, collapsing down to a single point of light that then shot up, the water erupting as though a fountain had just formed.

Just a single stream of water broke through, then the waters settled down again, dark and silent.

Shimokoro found himself smiling again. This time, he didn't bother changing his expression back to his usual, solemn mien.

The time had indeed come.

The fruit of all their plans had finally ripened: All of the careful manipulation, all the influence the House of Pearl had exerted, not just in the House of Cobalt but with all the houses, all the temples, ensuring that the right, or perhaps the exact *wrong* individual was in a place of power when the time came.

Maybe he would live to see all the lands ruled by a single LandHolder, the House of Pearl in ascendance.

And though the news was exciting and he wanted to tell the others of how the great plan was coming to fruition, he still made himself squat down beside the pool, waiting and spinning out more plans as the waters slowly drained away.

Chapter Five
HOUSE OF CRYSTAL

✦

AKALINA STOOD JUST inside the entrance of the dining room for the ghost court, dressed in her cobweb gown. Fine white lace flowed from her neck down to the dusty, ash-covered wooden floor. Her gown covered her white silk slippers, as well as hung past the tips of her fingers.

Maybe by the end of her year of attendance the thing would actually fit and she wouldn't look like such a little girl, dressing in her mother's clothing, despite the fact that she was almost fifteen.

A white ribbon tied just behind her ears held her long black hair away from her face, but the rest of it had been left loose and flowed down her back, a welcome warmth in the cold room. Her maid had applied fine white powder to her face that morning, as usual. She couldn't ask for reddened lips or cheeks, not until she had started her menses.

She hated resembling the ghosts she attended, but there was nothing she could do about it. Hopefully soon her status would change. But even if it was next week, it would still feel like months and *months* from now.

May as well be forever. That was how it felt sometimes.

She waited as she'd been trained to wait, patiently and silently, while the royal ghosts "ate" their midday feast. She'd tried to make it a game, to see how still she could be, but honestly, there wasn't much fun to it. Just standing and waiting for something—anything—to happen.

Come midafternoon, when Akalina could take a break from her duties, she'd slip out of the palace to one of the inner courtyards where no one could see her and would race around and around in the weak winter sunshine like a crazed bird finally uncaged, bruising her wings against the hard stone and wood walls. She'd come back inside sweating despite the piles of snow.

In the meantime, she waited, as she had for months now.

Over a dozen ghosts had gathered that afternoon, seated on plain wooden chairs around the long table. Akalina had been told that as the year progressed, fewer ghosts would manifest, until right before the next ghost month later in the fall, when more would show up again.

It wasn't a feast for the living, with roasted haunches of pork, boiled potatoes, and the last of the summer berries made into vinegary jam. Instead, the table was full of silver candelabras each holding dozens of candles. The candles themselves had been specially made so they smoked heavily. In the center of the table, a long carved piece of blood-red onyx held several pieces of crystalized copal incense, adding to the haze in the room but sweetening it considerably.

Beyond the table, narrow windows made from frosted glass and lead panes only allowed dim light into the room. Akalina would open them once the feast was over, air out the room so that the next group of feasters would not complain about "leftover" smoke. No pictures lined the plain wooden walls, no adornments were carved into the wooden chairs.

The ghosts had no taste for such things, so the room felt as stark as a crypt.

One that Akalina was buried in.

At the table, the ghosts waved themselves with round fans resembling small clam shells that came from the far away oceans, "drinking up" all the smoke.

One of the older ghosts—Rosahaptu—raised her hand and beckoned Akalina forward.

Akalina had learned not to rush but to do everything slowly, gracefully. Her training was exhausting, which was partly why she ran so hard when she had free time. But it wouldn't do to cause more air currents. If she accidentally did, the other ghosts around the table would complain about her "stealing" their allotted amount of the offerings, possibly even to the priests.

Rosahaptu had the appearance of most of the rest of the ghosts, looking as if she had been sculpted out of living clouds. Because she was an older ghost, the whiteness of her appearance was tinged with brown, which indicated her age. The younger the ghost, the whiter they appeared. Akalina had only seen one ghost older than Rosahaptu, an elderly gentleman whose smoke reminded her of an old parchment, his appearance more like a dust cloud.

The gown that Rosahaptu wore showed her neck and shoulders and barely contained her large breasts. Over a century ago, she'd been the LandHolder's consort. Her hair was curled pristinely around her face, while hairpins held the rest of it up. The pins jutted out all around her head, giving the impression of a crown. The originals must have been tipped in brilliant diamonds, as even in their ghostly form they still glowed.

The rest of Rosahaptu's outfit was less distinct. It took will to remain as a ghost, to not slide down into the underworld. Once there, a ghost had to play riddle games or be otherwise tested by a demon, set there by the Goddess Morta, before being allowed to find the River Guanaliki, then follow its course to the grand oceans of light and be carried away to the Golden Lands.

Some ghosts stayed in the lands of the living because they were afraid of the underworld, that they'd get stuck there, as many stories told of those who acted badly while they'd been alive. Other ghosts were afraid that the Golden Lands would reject them and they'd travel forever, lost on the oceans of light.

"More, dear," came the whispered request from Rosahaptu.

Though ghosts couldn't breathe, Akalina always thought Rosahaptu's breath smelled of lavender, which came from the sachets that had been used to preserve her body for viewing before it had been cremated in a magical fire.

Akalina understood what the ghost wanted. She slowly slid an arm forward and lifted one of the candles from a nearby candelabra. Then she used its flame to light one of the prepared but unlit piles of incense in the center of the table. She replaced the candle carefully, not spilling the scalding wax on her fingers as she had at the beginning of her time as an attendant.

At Rosahaptu's quiet sigh of contentment, Akalina withdrew to the side again. She couldn't just snap her fingers and cause a spark, though she knew that many in the Temple of Truth could. She'd tried. The only magic she had to speak of was her landsense, of always being rooted in the earth, knowing where she stood.

That, and the ability to listen to the ghosts, even when they weren't in the room.

It wasn't until she'd started her training as the attendant of the ghost court that she'd realized not everyone could hear their whispers, that few saw the weaker ghosts who were just shadows and not a full presence. Even her teachers didn't see the ghosts in every room of the palace, flowing in and out of the walls and windows, going about their ghostly business and not interacting with the living.

Akalina didn't remember when the ghosts had first come to her. They'd just always been there. She had a memory, though her older sisters told her that it couldn't be real, of lying in her crib and listening to a ghostly lullaby.

As Akalina was of the Kinrathy clan and tenuously related to the current LandHolder, she wouldn't be sent to spend the rest of her days in a temple. All four of the major temples worked with ghosts, though the Temple of Truth and the God Djediese dealt with them the most.

However, Akalina had other duties and responsibilities to the House of Crystal, such as marrying well and producing more members of the House. She wasn't betrothed yet, though that might happen this summer, her parents picking the appropriate husband for her, making a strategic alliance as they already had for her two older sisters.

Akalina only hoped they'd pick someone kind for her. They'd delayed making their choice because of her assignment to the ghost court. She knew they were hoping to parlay her experience into a better match.

Better for them and their social circles in the court. Not necessarily better for her.

As the ghosts finished their repast, some of the younger, brighter ghosts merely faded away. The older ghosts, including a short, stout man whose smoke was the color of tea-stained linen, stood up from the table and walked away, either leaving through one of the windows or the inner door on the right that led to a staircase going outside.

Rosahaptu stayed standing beside her chair, waiting until the others had left. She'd done that before, wanting to talk to Akalina.

If Akalina could run away, she would. The old ghost, while nice enough, always wanted to talk about the past, how things had been during *her* time.

The living had a responsibility to be polite to the ghosts, as they could cause trouble if they felt ignored. However, they had so little wisdom or even interesting stories!

Akalina contained her sigh and walked over to Rosahaptu when beckoned. She hoped the old woman wouldn't talk too long. Akalina *really* wanted to get outside before the sun slipped away and it grew too cold, the shadows too dark.

"Age, dear?" Rosahaptu whispered, the words as soft as falling snow.

"Fourteen," Akalina answered truthfully, as her birthday was just two weeks away.

"So young," Rosahaptu said, looking disappointed at her.

Akalina didn't reply. She wasn't sure what the ghost meant, but that happened all the time. Ghosts didn't always make sense.

A whispering noise fluttered around her, like the wind ruffling the dark pine trees that filled the forest just beyond the walls of palace.

Akalina glanced over her shoulder, but she didn't see any other ghosts in the room. She still felt their presence, like a mound of snow had gathered just behind her and radiated its cold maliciously.

"Closer," Rosahaptu commanded.

That was unusual. Ghosts didn't like the living to stand near them. They didn't enjoy their cloudy selves disturbed by a solid figure.

Akalina stepped right beside Rosahaptu, looking up. The smell of lavender increased. Rosahaptu's own internally lighted clouds darkened. Akalina felt pressure at her back, like cold hands pushing her forward.

34

"We all must do what we must," Rosahaptu said, much louder than her usual whisper.

Before Akalina could ask what she meant, Rosahaptu stretched her hand out and placed it solidly on Akalina's womb.

The pressure at Akalina's back increased. She couldn't step back. Couldn't turn to the side. Couldn't slide away, no matter how impolite that might be. She was being held against her will.

Ghosts weren't supposed to be able to affect the living this way!

Akalina tried to scream but the ghosts ate all the sound before it could escape. She flailed her arms and tried to push away Rosahaptu's hand. However, her solid form sliced right through the ghost's pale arm.

It was like trying to push away fog. And Akalina had no magic to call flames or move chairs or do anything that could help her.

Rosahaptu's hand on Akalina's womb abruptly grew cold. It felt as though a knife made of ice was slicing through her skin, inserting itself deep within her body. The pain washed over Akalina, making her gasp and try to scream again.

Rosahaptu appeared to follow the cold blade down. Her form wavered until she was no longer distinct but merely a wavy cloud shape. Her color faded, purifying to clean white. The pain diminished, until it was just a pinprick against Akalina's skin.

A hushed sigh filled the room. Akalina jumped back. Her movement caused what little was left of Rosahaptu to dissipate.

Trembling, Akalina looked around the room. No other ghosts were present. No one had witnessed what had just happened.

Instead of going about her duties, Akalina ran from the

room. Who should she tell? Not her mother; she would advise Akalina to lie about it, pretend it had never happened. Her mother did that a lot. No, Akalina would find Haptomi, tell him.

Surely the priest would know what to do about the cold that lingered inside Akalina, threatening to freeze her solid.

Chapter Six
HOUSE OF COBALT

KINAKI STIRRED, restless on his deathbed.

That idiotic healer had tried to convince the LandHolder that he wasn't actually dying, that all he had was merely a winter cold. But he knew. Could feel it in the way that the land was ebbing away from him, like the tide retreating from the shore. The tips of his fingers were no longer firmly encased in good soil, his toes were now freed of the bedrock that had held them for so many years.

It just wasn't fair! Kinaki wasn't that old. He should have a dozen or more years left as LandHolder for the House of Cobalt. At least until he was seventy. But no, the Abandonment had struck him at age fifty-eight. Too young. In his prime, some would say. Still strong and hearty, able to wield sword and shield.

He'd been cold all summer, though. At night, he'd insisted on fires burning high in the fireplace in his sleeping chamber while most had windows wide open, hoping for a breeze to stir the humid air. They'd even added magically heated stones to the mantle and around the room, not that he'd been able to feel them.

Now…now he lay here on his bed. Zhula, his wife, had at least seen to the chamber, making sure that the room was clean and that he was presentable, if any should choose to visit him.

Few came. He didn't blame them. The air was stuffy and humid, overly warm. (It didn't make any sense to him that he could be both so cold and so warm at the same time.) The strange teas that the healer insisted Kinaki try, along with the supposedly curative incense the idiot burned, persisted at the back of his mouth, making every smell and taste tinny.

His bed chamber wasn't that luxurious, not for his position. Sure, the down mattress rested on a tall, iron bedframe, with a beautiful design of calla lilies shooting up both the head- and footboard. Zhula replaced his worn-out, familiar quilt with something much finer and warmer, the blocks done in a pattern of blue, black, and silver. All the cobwebs had been chased down from the tall corners of the room, and the white-painted walls had been scrubbed and bleached.

This room had always been Kinaki's retreat. Very few people beyond his wife and consort had ever seen the inside of it. The bed took up most of the space, though since he'd fallen ill, a sturdy wooden chair had been shoved in beside it. The single candle on the bedside table had been replaced with half a dozen lamps hanging from the ceiling and filled with phosphorous rock, magically lit and constantly glowing. Even the windows had been changed, the frosted glass panes covered with white felt to keep more of the cold out.

The healer had told Kinaki to rest. What was the point in that? His body would stop moving soon enough. Yes, there was that absurdity that his soul needed to prepare itself for the journey ahead. It had never made sense to Kinaki, though, to sleep now when he was still alive, just so he might do better when he was dead.

According to the priests, Kinaki's soul would first travel down, beneath even their deepest mines, into the underworld. There, he might or might not have many trials, challenged by the demons set there by the Goddess Morta. (Kinaki knew there would be severe tests awaiting him, particularly given the number of barbarian souls he'd dispatched to the underworld during his time as LandHolder.) After he fought his way through the underworld, he'd reach the River Guanaliki. His soul would rest and float unharmed on the gentle waters, eventually trickling out of the darkness and flowing into the oceans of light.

At that point, he was supposed to travel across the oceans of light directly to the Golden Lands, to spend all of eternity at peace. That had always sounded awfully boring to him. Maybe he could join the others who stayed on the oceans of light, exploring.

He'd find out soon enough.

The afternoon wore on. Kinaki tried to push himself up to sitting, but he no longer had the strength. A bell now sat on the bedside table. He could ring it and see who responded, who would raise his weakened body up, then put pillows behind his head.

He didn't want to admit that he was afraid to ring the bell. What if no one came? Better to be restless in his bed than to have his solitary fate blatantly shoved into his face.

He rolled over again and happened to glance at the solid wooden door, shut firmly against the cold.

Dark smoke appeared to seep under the threshold, coalescing into a large, spinning pool.

Had he fallen asleep and not realized it? Or perhaps even died?

He swallowed against a suddenly dry throat. The taste of tin made him think that this was really happening.

Had a magician sent a shadow to harass him unto death? That seemed, well, rude. Not as if he knew of any magic like that, except in stories.

The smoke thickened. It brought with it the foul stench of an open grave, where bodies had been piled high and left to rot in the bright summer sunshine.

Like the bodies of the barbarians Kinaki and his warriors had killed.

A figure grew out of the pool. It towered at the end of Kinaki's bed. The form was man-like, though Kinaki couldn't see it clearly, as the edges of the smoke wavered.

LandHolder.

He knew the word hadn't been spoke out loud. He'd heard it through some other sense. Maybe he'd breathed it in along with the foul stench that turned his stomach, or absorbed it through his cold skin.

He nodded at the figure. Of course, the priests got the myths wrong. This was the being meant to escort him through the underworld, a treacherous companion meant to test his soul's mettle.

Do you want to live?

Kinaki jolted in his bed. If he'd had the strength to sit up, he would have.

Maybe this wasn't his escort. Maybe it was his second chance.

"How?" Kinaki asked. He didn't care how thin his voice sounded or how it cracked on the single word.

The creature raised an arm and directed Kinaki's attention to the side of the bed. More smoke rose up and coalesced into tiny figures playing out a scene.

It showed the LandHolder and the creature merging, becoming one. Kinaki would gain more power, much more, because his reach would extend beyond the land and into the underworld.

Following his ascension, there would be many battles. The other LandHolders fell beneath Kinaki's sword. Soon, he had all the land under his sway, a single LandHolder instead of four.

And all the underworld would be at his beck and call as well.

Only once before had all four lands been in control of a single LandHolder. There were conflicting stories of that time. Some said it had been a time of great peace, while other told of great conflict.

Through most of the centuries, the land had been split between as few as two LandHolders or as many as six.

Kinaki narrowed his eyes. He'd learned long ago that anything too good to be true generally was.

"What do you get?" he said, proud of how rock solid his voice sounded, instead of pleading and begging to be given this chance.

Air.

That made sense to Kinaki. The fresh air of the lands was enticing. He loved going up into the mountains to breathe in the greenery there, or stepping into one of the mines and smelling the good solid earth.

Everyone knew that the dead could breathe—how else could they inhale the smoke or incense burned for them?

"And?" he demanded. There had to be something else that this creature wanted, more than just the ability to breathe again.

Power it finally admitted.

Kinaki had the sense that the being craved power, the feel of all the land, as much as he did. But the power wouldn't be flowing in a single direction, like a strong river current. Instead, while the power of the land seeped into the creature, the power of the underworld would be Kinaki's to command.

He turned his head to the side, looking at the smoke

tendrils floating there, like small eels, waiting to do their master's bidding. "Show me again," he said.

He peered intently at the show, the pictures of how he and the thing at the foot of his bed would merge.

Would it still be him after the procedure? Would he still have control?

He nearly snorted at himself. Of course he would. No matter how much this thing might believe it had command of Kinaki, it had never met as stubborn of an individual as he.

Kinaki would be the primary will controlling their shared body.

Finally, Kinaki turned his stare back to the blackness pooled at the foot of his bed. He didn't try to bargain with the thing or to seek reassurances. That was for the weak and unsure. No, he would dominate it, the underworld, and soon, all the land.

"Come," Kinaki said. He focused his will and raised a trembling hand toward the creature. He couldn't hold it up for long, and it fell back onto the mattress like a dead thing.

The cold of the underworld flowed over Kinaki's soul and he took his last free breath.

Chapter Seven

HOUSE OF GOLD

UNNIR SAT STIFFLY on her throne in the court. She'd sat in session all day long, listening to arguments and passing judgments. Her bones felt creaky in the cold. Though she wasn't that old—barely in her thirties—somedays the winter winds blew daggers down her lungs and made her right hip ache (stupid childhood injury). Snow still clung to the mountains in the east, unwilling to retreat even an inch. Dark clouds chased each other across the sky, holding in the cold.

The room was huge, much larger than what she needed most days to hold her court. However, this was also the room where celebrations were held—births, deaths, weddings, coronations, and feasts for the various gods. The walls were solid granite, rising up twenty-five feet, with beautiful fluted columns along the edges to give the vaulted wooden roof strength. Gold had been inlaid into the walls in delicate geometric patterns that shimmered in the candlelight. Large white marble tiles, veined with black and gold, made up the floor.

Statues of the four gods lined one wall: the tall proud

Goddess Morta who brought both life and death, the smiling Goddess Orolorg, who made the land fertile and aware, the God Xiuma sitting fat and happy on his throne, bringing luck and wealth, and the God Djediese wrapped in his rainbow cloak, whose touch brought both magic and justice.

Usually, Unnir loved this room and its formal elegance. On days like today, none of the braziers burning in the corners could bring enough warmth to the cold stone.

The court stood before the LandHolder. It was one of the many things from her uncle, the former LandHolder, that she'd kept: making her supplicants stay on their feet so maybe they wouldn't argue as long.

She sat on a beautiful living throne, a honey locust tree grown specifically for her seat. The roots of the tree went far down into the earth, fed by the aquifers there. Thorns stuck out from the sides and back of the chair, six to eight inches long, sharp and deadly. Currently, the tree was bare of leaves, though Unnir could force it to bloom at any time. She tended to keep her throne in sync with the seasons, enjoying the bright green leaves and the strong scent of the tiny cream-colored flowers that would appear in the late spring, the long brown pods with their honey-like pulp at the end of summer, and how stunning the bright yellow leaves looked in the fall.

It was the second month of the year and too soon for even buds. So the tree stood, as ancient and as prickly as Unnir's mood. She wore gray that day, the iron-hard color of storm clouds. Black embroidery circled the long cuffs and decorated the front plaques. Braids held her golden-red hair tightly across her scalp and down her back. Gold rings rested on every finger, warm and heavy.

Though the people standing before her wore long solemn green robes, dressed in all the colors of the spring leaves, they seemed gray as well, as though she was looking at them through a dirty window.

Could she just interrupt the two currently arguing in front of her? Stand up and declare that court was over for the day?

Not without causing controversy. They'd wonder what was wrong with her, if she was pregnant again (no) or if she was sick (also wrong). She had to be careful of any action or indication that she was weak. She hadn't been in the position of LandHolder for even a full year, and at least half of that time she'd been pregnant with her littlest girl.

No one had expected the land to choose Unnir. Everyone had thought that one of her uncle's sons, Emil or Vide, would have inherited instead. Particularly when her uncle was accidentally killed, thrown by a new horse he'd been breaking in.

Though as LandHolder her uncle could ease many hurts, not even he could fix his own broken neck. When he'd died, the land had instantly sought out Unnir, wrapping itself around her like a wet cloak.

She had never trained to rule the land, not like Emil and Vide. She felt as though she was constantly being judged weak and unworthy of the House of Gold.

Too bad that the choice was permanent. There wasn't anything that the court could do, short of killing her. It brought a cold comfort to her sometimes.

Mostly, though, she ground her teeth in vexation at being unable to make any decision without severe consequences.

It didn't help that Torja, the head priestess of the Temple of Truth, was perceived to be a foolish young woman, even though she was at least six years older than Unnir.

And though the merchants and the farmers may be jockeying for more of Unnir's time, it was the warriors who concerned the LandHolder the most.

Barbarians—the general term that was used to describe those outside the land who had no landsense—lived east of the mountains. They'd made a concerted push in recent years to attack the houses and the lands on the western side, even going so far as to spill into the foothills and ravage the farms there. Her warriors, since they were no longer spending as much time defending the borders of the land from the other houses, needed something else to do. They wanted to push over the mountains to the east, to claim more land there in Unnir's name. Or for themselves.

Any perceived weakness from her and they might just go ahead and do that, with or without her blessing. Her damned cousins weren't helping. She couldn't say for certain, but she'd swear that they were agitating the VeinHolders, the leaders of the fighters, causing unrest among them.

Then what would she say to the other LandHolders when they met later that year? How would they take the news that instead of just defending her territory, she'd actually gone ahead and expanded it? They might insist that she give up some of land at her borders to make up for the newly acquired acres.

What if she couldn't hold onto any new territory? That was always an issue as well. The long mountain range to the east acted as a natural barrier for all of the houses. While it wasn't impossible for her to spread her landsense and rule that direction, it was difficult.

Unnir returned her attention to the two before her, FarmHolder Linged (head of the farmers) and MineHolder Ramford (head of the miners).

The Hold of Farmers (though, really, it was just a loose association of old men and women desperate to maintain their power and land) was insisting that the LandHolder (her) should do her annual Promenade of the fields early.

While the Hold of Miners was trying to demand her

attention first. After all, they were the ones who provided the gold for which her house was named. She should visit them before she did her annual Promenade.

It was all so tiresome! Couldn't they just leave her in peace?

Unnir finally realized that she wasn't giving anyone their proper due or her attention.

This wasn't good. She *had* to get out of there. It wasn't fair to either them if she couldn't actually listen.

"Thank you, both, for your thoughtful arguments," Unnir said in a loud voice, interrupting MineHolder Ramford from yet *another* round of whining. "I shall ponder what you've said and let you know the outcome of my judgment in the morning. For now, court is adjourned."

Stunned silence filled the room. She could hear it wafting out from her, billowing like fog and freezing all those who attended her.

"No, I'm not ill. Or pregnant. Something else has taken my attention away from you, though," Unnir said, letting her aggravation show.

"Very good, LandHolder. We shall adjourn and leave you to your meditation."

Unnir was surprised that the person supporting her was VeinHolder Daugny, head of the warriors. She stood in the darkest robe of the entire court, the green almost black, a dark shadow among all the lighter greens and golds.

"Thank you," Unnir said. "I shall come and sit in judgment again tomorrow, in the late morning."

With that, Unnir turned around, intending to go out one of the back doors behind the throne. When she strode forward, she realize her mistake. She hadn't swerved far enough to the side to avoid being scratched by the thorns sticking out from the edges of her throne.

Damn it! Her robe was caught. She shrank down the thorns, denuding her chair of them in her fury.

Crap. Her throne looked so vulnerable without its defenses.

She couldn't be bothered to grow them back just yet. It would be one more thing to do in the morning.

She stomped out of the throne room, knowing that she'd just shown herself to be weak, once again.

Chapter Eight
HOUSE OF PEARL

❦

DARIKUTO LISTENED to Shimokoro tell his tale once again, of the vision he'd witnessed three nights before. The small room they sat in felt crowded. This room was normally reserved for private meetings, just for himself as LandHolder of the House of Pearl and one other. Now, he was there with five other Holders, Shimoko, and Chuyoko, a tiny fierce woman who was the chief PearlHolder, the head of all the warriors.

If it weren't for the serious topic, the meeting might have been congenial, all of them sitting on pillows around a low table, knees and sometimes elbows touching. They'd partaken from the elegant sea-green carafe in the center of the table that contained fine plum wine, but now, they listened, the wine forgotten.

Solid walls surrounded the group, painted the creamy-white of finely rendered lard. No windows marred the pure expanse, no easy way for someone to listen in. Cool magical lights shone out of glass bowls that hung from chains in the corners. Two guards stood outside the solid door, women whom Darikuto trusted with his life.

The group met there, in the tiny room, with the wine, as a diversion. Just old friends getting together to chat. Or so he would have explained it to anyone who had asked.

Not holding the most important meeting of his long career as LandHolder.

Rumors and spies abounded in his court. He would just as soon not give them any more tidbits about The Plan.

That was how he thought of it. The Plan, which his father had initiated in his wisdom, may he live forever in the Golden Lands.

The Plan that would, step by step, create a single Land again, ruled by a single LandHolder.

The Plan, which was finally coming to fruition.

It had taken a lot of time to bring everything to this point. Gold and favors as well—more than he wanted to calculate. First, to bring peace and lull everyone into a sense of ease. To ensure that all the warriors except his own had lost their edge. Bribes to guarantee that those who'd been appointed to the Temple of Truth were weak. More bribes to sway the merchants and other guilds to favor the House of Pearl in obvious and unobvious ways.

There wasn't anything anyone could do to influence the choice of the LandHolder. Those Holders were chosen by the Land itself.

Unless there was no one appropriate.

It had happened in the past—entire families wiped out so that an already existing LandHolder might step in and coax the land to accept them instead.

Despite not being able to influence the selection of the other LandHolders, the ones currently in power were nearly perfect in terms of The Plan. It was as if the land itself, wanted The Plan to succeed. He'd had the luck of the God Xiuma, that was certain.

He only had to point to Unnir to make his point. No

one had expected her to inherit when her uncle died. It honestly had been an accident, though one that Darikuto called fortuitous, as it had allowed him to bring forward some pieces of The Plan.

Unnir was inexperienced and weak, and would soon be pregnant again. She would be easy to sway. Particularly since Torja, the head of her house's Temple of Truth, was rough and untrained, incapable of dealing with the subtleties of the court.

Kinaki had succumbed to the demons of the underworld. The poison he'd been fed with almost every meal had worked its magic, numbing his extremities and weakening his limbs, mimicking the feeling of the Abandonment despite the fact that Kinaki was still young and strong. Belam had called the demons forth thinking that he'd be able to control them, believing the fake text that Benitoyo had sold him. Now that Belam was dead, it would be much easier to control his replacement.

Haptomi was a fussy old fool who wouldn't advise the necessary bold moves to save the House of Crystal, but rather, would be conservative. Ibitsima was the only strong leader remaining. It had been much more difficult to poison her—they'd only succeeded in feeding her a little bit of it before they'd been caught out.

No matter. Darikuto had made the necessary adjustments to The Plan and would deal with her soon enough.

When Shimokoro finished his retelling, Darikuto spent a few moments looking around the room, catching the eye of each of those who sat with him at this turning point.

They all returned his look with resolve. Good. None of them were backing down.

"It will take some time before the corruption seeps out of the House of Cobalt," Darikuto said. "While everyone will notice that Kinaki has changed, no one will guess the true nature of his transformation. Belam's replacement, Sunli, is firmly in our pocket. He thinks he acts of his own accord and for the good of his house. But he, like Belam, has been fooled."

"How long before the next step?" Chuyoko asked. Almost everyone else nodded, as if she'd asked the question they all had in mind. She was a warrior, a woman of action, and fanatically dedicated to the LandHolder.

Darikuto shrugged. That was the most difficult aspect of The Plan to get across to the others. The Plan didn't have a timeline. It wasn't bound by months or years. It was driven by *events*. First this had to occur. It didn't matter when. Only then, could they take the next step.

"If I had to guess, two years," Darikuto said. The frowns he received for that response didn't surprise him, though in his heart of hearts, it did disappoint him.

His father had long taught the importance of patience, particularly once The Plan had started to come to fruition.

It was a lesson that for some reason, Darikuto had taken to readily. So few others did, though.

"This is the most crucial time," Darikuto warned. "If we are not careful, the other LandHolders will turn against me and not Kinaki. Or the underworld will conquer the world of the living."

Though no one at the table gave a physical shiver, he knew that in their souls they all felt the cold winds of death. It had been one of the largest risks of The Plan, to bring the underworld to their world, to get Belam to believe that he could control such forces.

It would be their greatest task to force those demons back below ground again.

"The threat must be allowed to manifest so that everyone will rally to our side," Darikuto continued. "We must wait until Kinaki makes the first move against Unnir. Then, and only then, can we offer aid. As well as deal that fatal blow to the House of Crystal."

Darikuto watched Chuyoko don her patience as though it were a coat of armor. She gave him a sharp nod. "We will be ready, whenever you say the word."

The others around the table made similar commitments. They would support him to the bitter end. Not only because they hoped to be rewarded in this life, but so that they might also gain favor in the Golden Lands.

How many of them would meet their end sooner than they'd expected? Probably all of them.

Darikuto had Plans for the other Holders as well, those who knew of The Plan. He didn't want them to blab about their participation afterward. It was to be him who got all the credit, he who would control all the Land.

No, those five Holders would all be fighting for their lives at some point. Demons and creatures from the underworld manifesting in their courts.

Fighting—and losing.

All to the glory of The Plan.

Chapter Nine
HOUSE OF CRYSTAL

IBITSIMA SAT in her morning chamber, sipping her peppermint tea and looking out over the winter gardens. The walls of the small room were painted a bright yellow, a cheery color that always improved her mood. Though two other chairs crowded around the round table in the center, for the time being, Ibitsima sat alone, musing.

The new year was waxing, as it were. Warmth was flooding back into the land, chasing away the snows, slowing waking the land from its long winter sleep.

As the LandHolder for the House of Crystal, Ibitsima felt the winter more than most. Ice settled along her back when she slept. She dreamed of the deep snow in the mountains to the north, of the winds slipping across frozen rivers, of the lumbering bears and other creatures still hibernating.

Lately, she'd even woken with her toes and fingers chilled. That hadn't happened in any of the previous five winters, since she'd come to power. Taranaptu, her husband, complained laughingly about how she was determined to be contrary, coming to bed warm and waking up cold, no matter how many blankets, furs, and comforters were piled up.

As the LandHolder, she could affect anything from her land that she touched. She could bring a dead plant back to life by running her fingers along its leaves. Smooth out a twisted branch and carve a design in it without tools. Revive an ailing well by visiting it and clearing out the debris far below the earth that had clogged the waters.

Normally, she would hold her cup—made out of a beautiful purple stone with white lines shot through it, carved from a geode dug out of her land—and warm it, thereby warming the contents within it.

However, the cold had lingered that morning. She had heated her tea using a small candle instead of her hands. The external heat sank into her skin slowly, as if her body was resisting such a force.

It couldn't be because she was getting old. Older, yes. She was forty now. She'd inherited from her father, who'd released his hold on the land when he'd been sixty-two, five years before. He'd died less than a year later, which wasn't that unusual. What had been different was that he hadn't died of the Abandonment—the wasting disease that sometimes struck those with landsense, when their sense of the land failed. Instead, it was a cold that had lingered, stealing his breath, that wouldn't respond to any magic.

She also had the feeling that he'd died sad, possibly heartbroken about something.

While Ibitsima had been raised during the times of war, she'd only reigned during peaceful times. Her father, on the other hand, had known war for most of his life— LandHolders fighting for territory, pushing their boundaries across each other's land, as well as fighting the barbarians who were trying to invade.

She didn't understand why she thought of her father that morning. His last words still puzzled her.

He'd told her, "People are more important than land."

What did that mean? How was that possible? People were replaceable. More would be born all the time. They could be trained, manipulated, misled.

While the land was...the land. It existed before the Goddess Orolorg had given birth to all the creatures and plants that lived on the earth, and would survive long after Ibitsima's entire clan had returned to the Golden Lands.

Before becoming a LandHolder, Ibitsima didn't understand the constant wars, why the LandHolders had fought for more territory, despite working with her father for years on various campaigns.

Once she felt the mantle of power resting on her shoulders, she suddenly knew.

The land she Held was wonderful. From the tall, snow-covered ranges to the north, through the dark trees and into the gentle meadows. The rivers and streams full of fish. The fields of golden millet and red barley.

She wore the land as she wore her body. She sometimes dreamed that she just had to reach out her hand to touch the faraway hills. She could feel the fish in the rivers slipping between her toes. The deep roots of the trees tangled in her hair.

But she also felt the need to stretch. Every morning, she awoke with her fingers cramped, as if she needed just a little more space. If she pushed out with her feet, her toes would run against a barrier.

More land would scratch that constant, irritating itch.

However, Ibitsima honored the hard-won accords that her father and the other LandHolders had put into place so that the wars would stop. Border disputes were rare now, even when a LandHolder passed, which had always been the time of most contention in the past.

Unnir had taken her Land without any battles, the first in recent history.

Before, warrior farmers would be gathered at the border, ready to push into the adjoining land as the current LandHolder ailed. They would bring with them the sense of their own house. Once settled across the border, it would be difficult for the new LandHolder to oust them. Thus the new LandHolder would lose territory, one farm at a time.

And that itch to acquire more land would grow stronger.

Since the peace had been struck, the four LandHolders met annually at a summer festival. The occasion was always hosted by a different house. The previous year, the festival had been in her lands, and the House of Crystal had entertained faraway guests for weeks of celebrations, parties, planning, and scheming.

This coming summer, Ibitsima would travel with most of her court to the House of Gold, the closest of any of her rivals, just south. The following festival would be held at the House of Cobalt, then the House of Pearl, then back to the House of Crystal.

Who would be at the next gathering of LandHolders? Would Kinaki, the LandHolder from the House of Cobalt, still be around? Ibitsima's spies had passed along rumors that he'd been ailing. It would be hard to deal with a LandHolder who had no experience with the land. They'd all suffered through that the previous year with Unnir.

While Ibitsima's three children always accompanied her to the summit, there was no guarantee that the land would choose one of them as the next heir. It was to be expected, of course. Most of the time, that was how the selection went. Ibitsima did what she could to encourage the land to pick one of her direct heirs. She sent her children down into the

Chamber of Crystals on a regular basis, in the hopes that the spirits who lived there would come to recognize them. She also had them traverse the borders of the land, as she had as a child, going on the annual Promenade.

It was good training for them to meet with their potential rivals and allies regularly. They were all of an age now, her youngest having just turned thirteen, her eldest eighteen.

Yet, none of them had ever been chosen to serve at the court of the ghosts. That was worrisome. Instead, a distant cousin had been selected that year. Akalina.

Something had happened to the girl the day before. Something big enough that Haptomi had insisted that both of them come to see Ibitsima in her chambers that morning.

Ibitsima shook her head, trying to clear away her winter dreams, the cold finally starting to seep out of her fingers and toes.

Why was she always so cold this winter? It couldn't be the Abandonment. Not yet. No, something else was at play.

But what?

❀

IBITSIMA LISTENED to Akalina tell her tale of the ghost touching her belly, how cold it had gotten, how it ached still. How she'd been held against her will, unable to turn away.

There was no precedent for this. Ghosts could aid the living, guide them by telling stories of what the future might hold, or past events that were similar. They could also vex them, mislead them with fables and myths.

However, the dead could not touch the living. She'd never heard of such a thing.

Haptomi stood behind the girl, as prim as always, wearing his best ivory and gold robes that covered him completely. The high collar complemented his stiff neck. Ibitsima had tried to get Akalina to relax, but the girl was too afraid. She still wore her cobweb dress, her face nearly as white as the lace. It was too big for her, the sleeves flowing past her wrists and the skirt dragging on the floor.

We all must do what we must.

Ibitsima had no idea what those words meant. She knew who Rosahaptu had been when she'd been alive. The LandHolder had been married and fathered his heirs with his wife, maintaining his allegiances and fulfilling his duty. But his true love had been Rosahaptu, whom he'd treated like a major Holder even though she had no land to speak of and not enough landsense to hold it.

She'd held his heart, and that had been enough.

Reading between the lines of the dry history about that time, Ibitsima had assumed that Rosahaptu had been bucking for the role of wife for most of her life. Though she wielded great power in the court, she never had the prestige of an important title.

And now, she was possibly gone. She had not come back to the ghost court that evening, though she generally showed up for every feast.

Had she used all of her essence in order to do something to Akalina?

After the girl had told her tale, Ibitsima questioned her for a while. However, the girl had no idea what had happened to her, what had been done to her.

"May I touch you?" Ibitsima asked quietly.

Akalina's eyes grew wide and she silently nodded.

Ibitsima reached out and placed her thankfully warm hand on the child's abdomen. While Ibitsima could sense the land all around her, people were a mystery. As LandHolder, she could frequently heal small ills. Proper healers were better at it, honestly.

Her father had been better at it, too.

Still, Ibitsima felt something there. Almost as if a second presence had taken root under the girl's skin.

"Have you started your menses?" Ibitsima said, drawing her hand back and rubbing her fingers together, trying to figure out what it was that she'd just felt.

"No, ma'am," Akalina said. "I'm not late," she added hastily. "My mother and her gran didn't start until they were nearly sixteen."

Ibitsima nodded. Her family had the trait of girls starting to breed early, but having that cycle end early as well. It was why her sister was so close in age to her, as her parents had decided to have children as quickly as they could.

"Do the ghosts seem different now?" Ibitsima said. "Since Rosahaptu touched you?"

Akalina shook her head violently.

Ibitsima recognized guilt when she saw it. Her own children had the same habit of denying the truth vehemently.

"So the ghosts don't seem different to you now," Ibitsima said. "Were they different before?"

Akalina bit her lips together.

"Tell her, girl," Haptomi said, his voice harsh and cold, particularly in the warm morning room.

Ibitsima wished that she could have held this meeting without the priest, but he would have taken it as a slight. As LandHolder, she was the supreme leader of the House of Crystal. However, she needed the support of the Temple of Truth, and it wouldn't do her any good to antagonize the head priest, as much as he might irk her sometimes.

"I can hear the ghosts, ma'am," Akalina said. She bent her head and studied the ground. "All the time."

"Have you always heard them?" Ibitsima said.

"Yes, ma'am. Even when I was a baby. They sung me lullabies," the girl admitted.

"Ah," Ibitsima said. She understood now. Akalina had always been in tune with the ghosts. If her family had merely been well connected and not part of the LandHolder's line, she would have already started training for the priesthood. They dealt with the ghosts, more so than Holders.

Akalina looked back up at Ibitsima, her lips pressed together firmly. Ibitsima knew that Akalina might have said something more if they'd been alone. However, Akalina wouldn't say anything else in front of the priest.

"That is all, then. I may call on you later, though," Ibitsima said, dismissing Akalina. She might ask the girl to attend her in a day or two. Without Haptomi.

After the girl had left, Ibitsima poured herself some more tea before glaring at Haptomi. "Sit, already," she said, pointing to one of the other chairs. "I don't need to get a crick in my neck looking up at you."

"Of course, ma'am," Haptomi said, sitting down. He held himself strictly upright, sitting as stiffly as he had been standing.

Ibitsima remembered her father once complaining about Haptomi having a stick rammed in an inappropriate place.

She'd never lost that opinion of him, quite frankly.

"What do you think of these events?" Ibitsima asked, sipping her tea. She didn't bother offering him any. He'd never accepted in the past and she didn't see any reason for him to change his mind now.

"I don't even know how to phrase the question for the chamber," Haptomi whined. "I can't ask what happened. I need to phrase it so the chamber replies with a name."

Ibitsima nodded. "Maybe ask who aided Rosahaptu?" she said.

"I don't know how that will help," Haptomi said, his tone verging on disparaging. "It isn't as if we could banish those ghosts from the ghost court."

"True," Ibitsima said. There was no magic that she was aware of that would hold ghosts at bay if they were intent on entering a room. Fortunately, by keeping a separate "court" for the ghosts, they rarely went anywhere other than the feasting hall that had been prepared for them. This usually meant they didn't bother causing any mischief.

While the ghosts lived in all the lands, they'd always been the strongest and most numerous in the House of Crystal. No one knew why. No one else had a ghost court—they didn't need one.

"However, by learning if Rosahaptu had accomplices, we might be able to figure out who had been working with her," Ibitsima said. "If it was her peers who helped, or ghosts of many ages." That would give them some idea of how big the plot was.

Haptomi frowned at that, but Ibitsima knew that he'd do as she requested.

"What is your interpretation of this event?" Ibitsima said after a bit, thinking about the shifting alliances in her own court.

"Isn't it obvious?" Haptomi said. "She's to be the next LandHolder. She's been chosen by the ghosts as the one to lead."

Ibitsima nodded. Most LandHolders had a better sense of the ghosts than a mere Holder did. The Chamber of Crystals had chosen Akalina to serve the ghosts. Now, the ghosts had touched her.

The girl was certainly being groomed to do something. But what?

"I will start including her in the formal affairs of the house," Ibitsima said. "When her year of service to the ghosts is over, she will go on Promenade with my own children."

Haptomi almost smiled at that. "Very good, ma'am."

After the priest had left, Ibitsima continued to sit in her

morning rooms, contemplating the true meaning of Rosahaptu's actions.

Ibitsima didn't believe that Akalina was suddenly pregnant, a virgin birth caused by the ghosts. Any creature brought about from such an event was surer to be monstrous as well as unviable, as the ghosts couldn't bring anything to life.

There was more than one story about the ghosts killing things, whether it be the grass in a courtyard, small birds who had important news for the LandHolder, or even the cracking of the hearthstones of a home.

Had the ghosts just killed something in Akalina? If so, what?

Chapter Ten

HOUSE OF COBALT

Sᴜɴʟɪ ʜᴜʀʀɪᴇᴅ on his way to his meeting with Benitoyo, the head merchant from the House of Pearl. He was glad to see that the servants kept even the back hallways clean, though the rugs on the floor were worn and the pictures that hung unevenly along the tall wooden walls were old-fashioned.

As the new head priest of the Temple of Truth, he could have insisted that Benitoyo meet him anywhere. Even come to his chambers later that evening.

However, Sunli was still feeling his way through his new responsibilities. And he was used to making his way to Benitoyo's quarters using these hallways. He justified it to himself as a method of keeping his fingers on the pulse of the palace. Dust had accumulated in the corners when the LandHolder Kinaki had first taken to his bed, showing that even the lesser servants were worried about losing their LandHolder.

Just a word from him, though, had cleaned up those passages right away.

Belam's death had come as quite a shock, though there

hadn't been any evidence of anyone other than the priests and priestesses of the Temple of Truth feeling the loss.

Sunli knew that he'd never forget the last time he looked on Belam's face. Though there were no obvious marks on the body, he'd died with his mouth frozen in a scream of fear, his eyes wide open in terror.

It hadn't just been smoke inhalation that had taken Sunli's mentor. Most came to accept that it had been the augury that he'd been attempting that had frightened him to death.

Sunli happily accepted that it had just been the augury responsible for Belam's death, that he'd drawn it down on himself as well as ruined the augury room. Even the door no longer shut properly! Sunli had already begun looking at plans for a new room to be dug into the basement of the palace.

But Belam's face kept haunting him.

At least there had been some good news. Right about the time Belam's body was found, Kinaki had risen from what some had privately been whispering was his deathbed. The LandHolder appeared to be miraculously regaining his strength. Just that morning, three days after leaving his bed, Kinaki had spent time in the courtyard with the warriors, going through their morning stretches.

Sunli hadn't bothered watching. He'd sent his assistant Junra to witness the miracle instead. She'd reported that it wasn't until the end of the warmup that Kinaki's fingers had started trembling. They both took that as a good sign, that despite Kinaki's month-long illness, he was recovering his strength quickly..

She'd also commented on how Kinaki's bronze skin had a faint red tint to it now, as if he constantly ran a fever. But the healers couldn't deny that Kinaki was well again. They urged that he take it easy.

The LandHolder had actually laughed in their faces at the suggestion.

Benitoyo was one of the few outsiders who had a permanent residence at the palace. However, his quarters weren't necessarily in the most favorable quarter. His rooms overlooked the kitchen courtyard, which meant that he woke early with the banging of pans and the cursing of cooks every morning. When Sunli had delicately suggested that maybe Benitoyo could move to better quarters, or even outside the palace, the merchant had just laughed.

"They keep me on my toes," he'd said with a twinkle in his dark eyes. "Remind me of where I came from."

Sunli had appreciated that. Though his beginnings hadn't been that humble, he still made an effort to understand the little people, the servants who actually ran the palace, the warriors and their fierce pride, the artisans' flighty ways, even the farmers and miners.

It was going to be difficult to keep track of all those small details, now that he was the head of the Temple of Truth. But he was determined to manage it. That had been Belam's problem—too concerned with the future and potential sweeping changes and not paying enough attention to the smaller pieces.

Sunli knocked on Benitoyo's door when he arrived, punctual as always.

"Come in!" came the hearty response.

That was something that Sunli appreciated about Benitoyo: how exuberantly the merchant did everything. He attacked his meals with gusto, smacked his lips with appreciation while drinking his beer, entreating others to enjoy whatever entertainment he'd arranged for the evening.

He also mated lustily, and often, at least according to the rumors that Sunli had specifically paid for. His predecessor, Belam had not thought that those details were necessary, however, Sunli had wanted a more complete picture of the merchant before trusting him.

It was shocking, therefore, for Sunli to find Benitoyo ensconced on a new settee recently added to his front room, heavy blankets tucked in around him and pillows supporting his back. The room smelled of stale sweat and grassy tea, the kind always prescribed by the healers no matter what your ailment. The small fireplace in the corner had magically heated stones piled high. Sunli was already sweating.

"Ah, my friend," Benitoyo said warmly. "I am heartened that you have come, yourself, instead of sending a servant to fetch me."

"But of course!" Sunli said. He peered at Benitoyo. The man's skin was normally a dark brown color, not as ruddy as those who came from the House of Cobalt. The merchant looked pale that day as if he'd washed his face in ashes, his black eyes dull. He wore a long-sleeved nightshirt, the white stark against his face.

"What happened?" Sunli said, tugging one of the comfortable chairs and tugging it closer to where Benitoyo lay.

"Just a winter cold," Benitoyo assured him. "I'll be fine again in no time."

Sunli nodded, not trusting the glassy look in Benitoyo's dark eyes.

"Besides," Benitoyo continued. "It is the time of miracles. Kinaki has recovered. And you've finally reached your appropriate level."

"Thank you," Sunli said. He didn't always believe Benitoyo's flattery, but he did appreciate hearing it. "So how may I help you this morning?"

"I need you to clear up a rumor for me," Benitoyo said. His hearty voice dropped slightly.

Was he afraid of spies? Sunli didn't bother keeping track

of who visited the merchant—particularly not after they'd become friends. Or did Benitoyo not have the strength that he pretended? Had he dropped his voice because just this visit had left him weak?

"I've heard that Kinaki has already called on his warriors and the CollierHolders. There appears to be some concern about the barbarians to the south," Benitoyo said.

Sunli had heard the same rumors. In addition, he'd also heard speculation that Kinaki wasn't just focused on the south, but on the north as well.

Unnir's lands.

"I know that he met with the CollierHolders," Sunli said. "But primarily, it was so he could learn of all that had happened while he'd been sick. Nothing more."

Benitoyo nodded, smiling, as if hearing the cautious lie in Sunli's words. "So the warriors are not making plans to start amassing on the southern border?"

"None that I'm aware of," Sunli said. Of course, before they made such a move, they'd consult with the Temple of Truth to receive an augury that would guide them in their strategy. Or possibly the timing. The warriors would never act on their own without the temple. He was certain of it.

"You know I'm curious because I want to make sure that I have the appropriate supplies at hand," Benitoyo said with a determinedly large smile. "Don't want to be caught flat footed, unable to capture the market."

Sunli nodded, "I understand." When he fed information to Benitoyo that ended up with the merchant making a huge profit, a little of that windfall always came back to line his own pockets.

It wasn't bribery. Not really. It was just how the world worked. Sunli had been raised to be very practical. Benitoyo always showed his appreciation of a practical man.

"Thank you," Benitoyo said, his head falling back on his pillows.

"Is that all?" Sunli said, slowly rising after the merchant closed his eyes and lay breathing heavily for a while.

"Mmmm?" Benitoyo said. "Oh, please excuse my rudeness. I'm not as well as I think I am. I'm so sorry I made you come all the way here for just a simple question. But there was no one else I could ask, no one I could trust. Only you."

"It's all right, old friend," Sunli said. "I understand."

He quickly took his leave of the merchant's quarters and headed back to his temple using the same back hallway. He had many more meetings that day. So many details to process.

Still, Sunli felt uneasy, so much that his stomach was queasy with it. Kinaki had had the same look as Benitoyo when he'd first gotten ill, experiencing a general malaise and exhaustion, as well as feeling the cold much more acutely than others.

Would Benitoyo make the same miraculous recovery as Kinaki? Or would the merchant succumb to the illness? Particularly since this was not his land? He had some magic, of course, everyone did. But it wouldn't be that great outside of the land controlled by the House of Pearl.

Sunli wasn't sure if asking about Benitoyo's health was worthy of augury, but he might try it later that afternoon. As long as he was careful about it, not trying to reach too far. He wasn't about to attempt such a strong foretelling as Belam had. He didn't see the need.

No, he would never throw his life away like that. Belam's terror would haunt Sunli for the rest of his days.

Chapter Eleven
HOUSE OF GOLD

EMIL SPRAWLED in the tall chair set beside the roaring fire in his sitting room, stewing. The room was warm enough that he'd stripped off his long cloak and lounged in just a shirt and loose pants. His boots lay in a heap beside the door and he deliberately dug his bare toes into the thick wool rug so that he didn't jump up and do something, anything, to vent his anger.

Instead, Emil took another deep swig of the fortified wine sitting on the table beside his chair, the dark red burning its way into his belly, adding to his already overheated skin.

It wasn't just the air in his rooms that left him sweating, no, it was also his incredibly foolish cousin, the thrice damned *LandHolder* that the House of Gold had had foisted on them.

Why had *she* been chosen? You only had to take one look at her and you'd know how unsuitable she was. She was tall, like all of them. Her hair was blonde and her eyes were gray. But that was where the similarities ended. She didn't understand the land, didn't understand the court, didn't get that the merchants and farmers and everyone else expected her to *lead*, not to listen and then finally agree with whoever shouted the loudest. Or whoever had talked with her most recently.

The situation was untenable. Whatever favor the House of Gold might accrue hosting all the houses that summer was sure to dribble away. Worse, Unnir would leave opportunities lying on the ground like the gold in legend, strewn across the Miner Fields that their descendants first found.

Favors that others were likely to pick up and at some point, use against them.

Yudur, Emil's father, would never have allowed the arguments to go as long as Unnir had. He would have taken action. Bashed heads together.

It had been with the greatest reluctance that he'd accepted the peace accords. Emil knew that his father had plans, that he might have used this time to secretly gather his own warriors together, prepare them for a major push into unsuspecting lands. Like to the south, and the House of Cobalt, where Kinaki was ailing.

But no. Unnir wouldn't try to expand her borders by even an inch. It was disgusting. So like a woman, content with whatever crumbs that had been handed them.

A knock interrupted Emil's dark thoughts. "Come!" he called immediately.

Whoever it was had better have a good excuse for disturbing him or he was going to unleash his anger on them.

Vide came striding into the room.

Emil glared at him, then sighed. No matter how much he might want to berate his brother, he knew that if he did, it would at some point come back and bite him. While Emil was as good at fighting as any warrior, there was no denying that Vide could, sometimes, perhaps, be better at strategy.

And Vide could hold a grudge like no one else, not taking his revenge for an impressively long time.

"What do you want?" Emil said sourly, picking up his glass and taking another long drink.

Vide raised a single eyebrow at him, then with a wave of his hand, magically decreased the heat of the flames in the fireplace. "It was reported that you had a face full of thunder at dinner, my dear brother," Vide said. "So of course, I thought I should come to see what ails you."

"You know damned well what *ails* me," Emil said.

"Our cousin," Vide said, nodding.

"Our cousin," Emil said. He sighed, suddenly deflating in his chair. "You heard what she did this afternoon? Instead of solving the issue, she had to run away. Again."

"I did," Vide said. He gave his brother a grin. "And nearly impaled herself on her throne."

Emil snorted. That had been the only good news that afternoon so far.

"And what of the warriors?" Emil asked.

"They are still chomping at the bit, as it were," Vide said. "It wouldn't take much to push them that way, to get them to go settle old scores with the barbarians to the east. However, I'm not certain that is the wisest course."

Emil scowled at Vide. They'd gone around and around on this point. Using the warriors would be one of the easiest ways to show that Unnir was actually a weak leader, unfit to be the LandHolder as she was unable to control the VeinHolders and the warriors who reported to them. It would be a victory for them if Unnir was unable to hold any land they acquired.

On the one hand, the land had chosen her. On the other hand, she could always be banished. The court had risen up against Old Ennis, at least according to the legends, and forced him to leave. The priests and priestesses had all worked together, casting a terrible spell to strip the land from him. After a week or so, the land had chosen a different, more suitable leader.

Or they could kill her outright. The problem was that if the land was being finicky, it wouldn't necessarily choose either Emil or Vide to be the new LandHolder, particularly not if they'd actually assassinated Unnir. There were stories about that sort of thing as well, myths warning against it, how would-be assassins were suddenly Abandoned by the land, unable to sense it at all.

But if they could *prove* that she was incompetent, and get the court to turn against her, banishment did become an option. And their hands would be clean.

Surely the land would have come to its senses by then and would choose one of them this time.

"Then what do you propose if we aren't to use the warriors and the VeinHolders? How do we best illustrate for the court just how unfit she is?" Emil asked. His words came from deep in his throat, a growl of frustration.

"She must go on Promenade sometime this spring," Vide said. "How can we show her in the worst possible light to the half-witted farmers she visits? How do we get the miners as well to turn against her? Just using the warriors will only convince a few royals. No, we need to turn everyone's opinion against her."

Emil sighed. He knew that any negative comment he made would just get the common refrain of "you're not thinking big enough." Instead, he said, "So what's the plan?"

Vide looked surprised. "Given your current temperament, I had figured I'd lose at least an hour or more to convincing you that this is the most expedient way to remove this thorn from our side."

Emil shrugged. "No matter what we do, it's going to take time for us to enact this new plot of ours. It will be a year or more before it comes to fruition. Might as well get started now."

"My dear brother, where has this wisdom been lurking all these years?" Vide said with exaggerated astonishment.

Emil took another sip of his wine instead of replying. It had occurred to him that there wasn't a single thorn in his side but two: Unnir and Vide.

The land would choose a single LandHolder once Unnir was gone.

It wouldn't take much for Emil to show Vide's hand at the base of Unnir's demise. So if the land foolishly chose his younger brother, it wouldn't take long to get him banished either. Particularly since Torja didn't care much for Vide, and she'd probably be the one performing the majority of the ceremony.

Emil sat back in his chair, holding his fortified wine close to his chest while Vide took the chair beside him and started to spin his webs.

Chapter Twelve

HOUSE OF PEARL

CHUYOKO FACED A DARK SEA, her back to the dawn. Constant cold winds blew in her face. The smell of the ocean drenched her. The sand was soft under her hard boots, keeping her awareness in her toes, so she wouldn't accidentally slide.

She had already warmed up that morning, going through all the warrior positions, slowly moving from one to the next, pushing her hands from one side to the other and loosening up all her muscles. She did the long version, of course. This was not a time for shortcuts.

Once she finished her warmup, she bowed to the west, the place of power as far as the House of Pearl was concerned. She knew that others based their opinion about the importance of one cardinal point over another due to the location of their land and house. Therefore, it was traditional for the House of Pearl to venerate the west.

However, everyone was incorrect about why they thought west was vital.

West was the direction associated with the Goddess Morta, who both brought the storms and calmed the winds, the goddess of the moon whom most of the warriors prayed to. It was also associated with death—everyone knew that the Golden Lands lay to the west.

While life and land were important, *everyone* at some time faced death.

Chuyoko wore her medium armor that day. It was more for dress or show than for battle, though it would protect her. She would wear heavier armor when they made their way into the House of Cobalt territory, when it was time to do battle there.

The armor she wore today was made from many bands of thin, blackened metal sewn into a leather vest, protecting her torso. White paste formed into balls studded the seams, a poor man's pearls. While Chuyoko could afford real pearls, it didn't make any sense to her to put them on armor that was likely to get bashed.

Heavier, solid steel pauldrons protected her shoulders, and chainmail sleeves covered her arms. A thick steel girdle rode high on her hips, while more bands were sewn into the thighs of her pants. The solid boots she wore had steel plates in the toes as well as the heels.

Every day, Chuyoko faced the sea and the strong winds and practiced the warrior forms, dressed in one of her suits of armor, cycling through from her lightest to her heaviest set, then back down again.

Chuyoko was determined to be the most perfect warrior she could be. As she was shorter than almost all of the men she spared with on a regular basis, it was incumbent to be better than they were. Stronger. More fit.

She had to be ready when it was time.

Behind Chuyoko lay two different swords as well as a shield. She practiced with different weapons every day, ensuring that even if she wasn't the absolute best, she would be considered among the best. Swords, daggers, knives, pikes, and hammers. At least three times a week she also worked with both bows and crossbows.

That morning, she first drew her long sword out from its sheath. The blade was double-edged and just over three feet long. She remembered how unwieldly it had been the first time she'd drawn it, as she herself was just over five feet tall. The pommel was wrapped in shark skin and comfortably fit both of her hands, even with her gloves on.

Chuyoko stubbornly started to swing the blade with one hand, then the other. It was difficult for her to fight with such a long weapon using a single hand. However, she was determined not just to do it, but to do it well. She went through every strike and deflection as long as her muscles would support the weight, eventually switching to two hands to finish off all the positions.

After a short break, she drew the shorter sword and picked up her shield, going through every single fighting position.

Finally, when her thighs were shaking and her arms felt leaden, Chuyoko finished her practice. She put away her weapons and bowed low to the sea, the sun having risen maybe a hand's width past the horizon. She would jog to the palace at the heart of the city Yawatan with her weapons strapped to her back, eat breakfast with the rest of the warriors who were only now waking, then spend the day either sparring with the others or teaching. After dinner, she and the other PearlHolders would talk strategy, gaming out scenarios, putting new plans into place.

Eventually she'd crash, fall into a deep, restful sleep, then wake before the dawn and start all over again.

No one trained as hard as she did. No one had to, at least, not yet.

The Plan was slowly coming to fruition. Chuyoko didn't know all the pieces, just the most important one.

Kinaki had fallen prey to darkness.

Soon, she and her warriors would be involved in battles not just for the land but for their very souls.

It was her job to make sure that they were all ready. Darikuto was counting on her. She would never let him down, not while there was still strength in her body, breath in her lungs, a soul stirring in her belly.

She had sworn to follow him forever, even after death.

Chapter Thirteen

HOUSE OF CRYSTAL

❧❧❧

AKALINA STILL DIDN'T KNOW what had happened to her the previous year, when Rosahaptu had touched her belly. Ghosts were more distinct now. She saw them everywhere. They accompanied her through her day, floating in and out of her classroom where she studied with her sisters, followed her into the courtyard when she went to pick flowers for her mother, listened in as she gossiped with her maid.

Some claimed that there were fewer ghosts than before. Akalina didn't think that was the case at all. It seemed to her that while some of the ghosts were less present, more hid in corners than ever before.

When Akalina stopped to think about it, she still felt a sliver of cold deep inside her body, like a twig made of ice that had rooted itself in her belly. She didn't tell anyone about that. That was her secret.

Once every other month or so, Akalina was invited to have tea with Ibitsima, generally now without Haptomi. She told the LandHolder about her strengthened connection to the land. Akalina had always had a good sense of the land. Like her siblings and cousins, she could never get lost or confused about where she was, no matter how long she spun around like a little kid with her eyes closed.

This year, she felt the land around her waking up with the spring. The snow had melted early and the ground was alive. If she listened, she could hear the grass pushing its way out of the dark soil, a soothing rustling sound. Crocus buds made a popping noise as they reached for the air. Breezes carried more birdsong, the robins returning from their southern nests.

Ibitsima had seemed thoughtful when Akalina had first told her about her landsense. She didn't learn until later that her cousins, Ibitsima's children, didn't have as strong of a connection to the land as she did.

Akalina's magic had grown stronger as well. Over the last few months she'd learned how to snap her fingers and cause a candle to light or stones to heat. She drew soft winds effortlessly during the worst of the summer heat. It was easy to clear a path through the snow as well. She wasn't strong enough to move the earth or to heal the limb of a tree. Possibly she would be able to when she was older.

Haptomi considered her a viable contender for the land once Ibitsima passed. He treated her with a syrupy kindness at odds with his stiffness. Particularly since, after her year's attendance to the court of the ghosts, a different cousin was chosen—one of the older ones.

Still not one of the LandHolder's children.

Everyone treated her differently once she finished her year attending the ghost court. She had different teachers now, and always felt as though she was behind in her lessons. There was so much to learn! Not just history, and all the ballads and ancient poems, but names of all the important Holders, those living as well as recently passed.

Her parents still hadn't arranged for her marriage. Akalina knew they were bargaining with a very rich Holder currently, who'd been looking for a wife for his son. Akalina didn't like either of them, but she'd hold her peace and hope for the best. Surely her parents knew what was best. They'd done well with Befery, her eldest sister, who was eight years older than her. However, Pamosi, her middle sister, only three years older, had been married to a wretched man. She always looked so pale now, never smiling or happy.

That spring, Akalina had been invited to go on Promenade with the LandHolder as well as her three children. Akalina had played with all of them growing up. She and the one girl, Teseti, had even played "court" together, with each of them taking turns being the Holder and ordering everyone else around.

Since Akalina had attended the court of the ghosts, the three siblings had all grown cold and only talked with Akalina when they had to. They didn't need the adults explaining the consequences of Akalina being chosen to attend the court of the ghosts, the fact that she now attended more meals with them than with her own mother and father, that she was now on Promenade with them and being introduced to everyone.

Thankfully, the Holders were used to it, even outside of Nyati, the capital city. The House of Crystal had always trained many children to be leaders, unlike the House of Gold, whose LandHolder had only focused on his two sons.

That afternoon, Akalina had a little time to herself. She had wandered from the main hold, across an empty, open field, heading for a river tumbling with rushing water, full of freshly melted snow.

The river had called to her while she'd been having lunch in the hall. Though she knew that the land didn't actually have feelings like people did, it still felt as though the stream wanted to show off to someone who might marvel at its sparkling waters.

She wore a thick, black, wool coat that kept off the worst of the cold, as well as bright red mittens that her mother had given to her, knit from the softest rabbit fur. A matching red scarf tied around her neck made her skin itch slightly, but she didn't loosen it, preferring the tickling fur to the cold. At least she'd remembered to put on softer leggings under her wool trousers so they didn't itch as well. Her heavy boots kept her feet dry.

A muddy trail led along the bank of the river. The trees were still bare against the brilliantly blue sky, too early for buds. Sunlight shone through their branches, dappling the wet ground. Akalina walked upstream along the trail to a huge, tall rock that looked perfect for sitting on, jutting out of the side of the bank over the water. A cluster of boulders lay piled beside the jutting piece, as if the big rock had forced its way out of the earth and shouldered aside the stones that had once slumbered with it.

Akalina clambered over the boulders, slowly making her way to the top. It felt good to stretch and pull herself up using her muscles instead of the land to bolster her steps and help her with handholds.

When she pulled herself up to the top of the rock and stood, she stopped, startled, not walking to that spot a few feet away, to the tip of the rock.

Someone else had beaten her up to the top of the stone. As he was sitting on the far side, she hadn't seen him when she'd first looked up.

The young boy had dark hair that curled like hers and cool gray eyes looking at her steadily. He was dressed in very fine clothes—a brown wool vest over a thick linen shirt the color of dried mustard—so he was possibly one of the Holder's sons.

"Hello," he said gravely as she stood there swaying, undecided. "Did the river call to you as well?"

"It did," Akalina said, staying where she was, awkwardly shifting from one foot to the other. "May I join you there, watching it?"

The boy made a face, as if he'd just smelled something sour. But his words were spoken in a gracious tone. "Of course! Please, make your way up here."

"No, stay where you are," Akalina told him when she saw him starting to skootch to the side. "I can sit over here," she added, letting him keep the flattest and probably most comfortable spot up there.

"Do you come out to watch the river often?" Akalina asked.

The boy nodded, his attention firmly drawn back to the water rushing beneath them. "It's a really nice spot in the summer," he said finally. "When the trees have all their leaves. The rock is cool then, and the water makes it nicer."

Akalina nodded. They sat in silence for a while, listening to the stream, the spring winds still chilly but soft, not like the knife-edged winter gales.

"I'm Yimifut," the boy said after a bit. "Youngest to Holder Sitre."

"Akalina," she said. "Ibitsima is my aunt." That was all she really had to say to anyone. Most of the adults drew their own conclusions.

Yimifut nodded, his gaze taking in all of her. "You have a funny cloak on," he told her gravely.

"What cloak?" Akalina said. She wasn't wearing a cloak. Just a jacket, scarf, and mittens.

"It's like a white cloud," Yimifut said, nodding, "all around your shoulders and head."

Akalina shrugged. "What else can you see?" It didn't surprise her that someone from the Holder's family had an affinity for magic. Those with the strongest sense of the land had the strongest magic.

"Spread your arms out," Yimifut said.

Akalina obliging held her hands out to her sides.

"The cloak is tied together over your stomach," he said, pointing directly to the spot that Rosahaptu had touched.

Akalina couldn't help but shiver. "What else?" she demanded.

Yimifut pressed his lips together. "The priests in the Temple of Truth tell me I shouldn't talk about these things. That they aren't true. That the God Djediese isn't sending his attendants to help me see through the veils."

"I believe you," Akalina said. This boy knew nothing of her, and yet could see more than Haptomi or Ibitsima, she was certain of it.

"You have cold winds around you, too," Yimifut said. "Blue and white. They will keep you alive."

"What do you mean?" Akalina asked, alarmed now.

Yimifut shook his head. "I'm not supposed to talk about what I see," he said firmly, turning toward the water again, no longer looking at her.

That surprised Akalina. Though the major auguries in the lands of the House of Crystal came from visions spilled out of specially treated rocks and crystals, that didn't prevent individuals from having visions without holding them. The hero Banhefen had been captured by a rival house and tied up in a cave, and yet still had his visions and foretold his enemy's doom.

"What do you see?" Akalina said, a chill racing down her spine that was not caused by any spring wind. "You can tell me. I won't tell anyone else. I promise."

Yimifut remained silent, watching the water. It wasn't until Akalina got up to go that she thought he said, "You will live. No one else."

She didn't bother to ask more of his dire predictions. Perhaps the temple priests were right, and he shouldn't tell people what he saw, particularly if his visions were all about death.

Augury could never be completely trusted. Visions brought about through the crystals were true. However, there was more than one myth about how just a part of a vision was shone, and therefore how easy it was for a prediction to be misinterpreted.

Yimifut had to be wrong. Ibitsima and the others would survive. What could possibly kill all of them? Since she went everywhere with them, wouldn't she, too, be killed?

It made no sense. He was just being fanciful. Akalina hurried back to the Hold, determined to forget everything he'd said.

And she did, and didn't remember his warning until it was much, much too late.

Chapter Fourteen
HOUSE OF COBALT

Kinaki stood in the courtyard with the warriors, going through the general fighting forms and warming up his body. The demon Wanho—and Kinaki didn't lie to himself, he knew that he now shared his body with a demon from the underworld—didn't see the necessity of spending time stretching, either loosening their shared body's muscles or strengthening them. Wanho could do all of that for Kinaki through magic. Why waste time going through what were, at least according to the demon, boring exercises?

Kinaki still stubbornly went to the courtyard every morning and practiced since he'd recovered, well over a year before. The warriors expected him there. If he stopped, they would wonder, perhaps even believing that he'd gotten sick again, never guessing his true ailment.

Wanho allowed Kinaki his exercises, though the first few times Wanho had inflated Kinaki's muscles afterward, growing them like tumors. Kinaki had taken to wearing looser robes because he never knew what shape his body might be forced into by Wanho.

It was good that the demon only focused on maintaining

Kinaki's body and not speaking using Kinaki's mouth. The man was still stubbornly in control of his words, at least for the time being. Wanho seemed amused by Kinaki's insistence that he do all the talking. Of course, Wanho could cut off air or sound, making it impossible for Kinaki to say something. Fortunately, that didn't happen often.

Instead, they'd come to an agreement. Kinaki agreed to experience the sensual world for Wanho, introducing new tastes, smells, and sensations, while Wanho let Kinaki direct what they did for the most part.

Kinaki told himself that it was worth it. He counted every day that he remained in the land, every breath he took, as a win.

Even if the air always held the faintest tinge of smoke, no matter where he stood.

Wanho marveled at all the colors of the land, the brilliant blue of the sky, how bright and white the snow was on the mountains to the east and south, how richly black the earth was. During the first few months after they'd merged, the demon had insisted that they spend hours staring out the windows of the palace, looking out on the grounds.

It had surprised Kinaki that the demon had a love of flowers. Was it their color? Their fragrance, which almost cut through the constant smell of smoke? Flowers were sometimes used to honor the dead. Was that why the demon liked them so? Though had the demon at one point been alive? Kinaki wasn't sure.

Zhula had thought it was odd, but she'd arranged for fresh flowers to be put in Kinaki's bedchambers every morning. He told her that they reminded him that he was still alive.

More flowers had crept into the halls where he met with the Holders and the guilds. He'd commissioned a new set of armor, cobalt blue, of course, but with the pattern of a blue cornflowers outlined in white in the center of the chest.

He'd joked once that since he'd been reborn, his name should be The Flower LandHolder. Some in the court had taken up the name. The gardens around the back of the palace now held multitudes of exotic and beautiful flowers, gifts from various Holders. Kinaki walked through the garden paths often, the demon inside of him practically purring in delight.

Kinaki finished the exercises that morning and bowed with the rest of the warriors toward the south, the seat of their power, and the mines that held the precious minerals that gave the House of Cobalt its tremendous wealth. The air was still cool, though it would be warming soon. Spring had run its course and summer was eagerly waiting its turn.

Then Kinaki hurried from the courtyard back toward the palace as he saw two of his CollierHolders heading toward him. He had too much to do that morning to be waylaid by the leaders of his warriors.

He knew what they wanted to talk about. They felt they needed more support for their fighters in order to maintain the front to the west, against the barbarians. He hadn't bothered telling them that this "war" was merely a diversion. As those fighters were well away from the court, they could amass and train in secret. No one except Kinaki had any idea how many warriors he had actually accumulated in various training camps.

Soon, he would recall all of his groups of fighters—the PitHolders, the ShaftHolders, down to the smallest cadre of CinderHolders—and throw them in the opposite direction, against the House of Gold, expanding his territory there.

He would wait at least one more year, until the gathering of LandHolders in Yawatan, the House of Pearl's capital city.

Everyone's attention would be focused to the west, and he could quietly start secreting his warriors across the borders.

Wanho didn't see the point in waiting. Kinaki had plenty of warriors, armies that he hadn't called on yet—those from the underworld.

Kinaki had tried explaining the concept of surprise to Wanho, how it would be much more effective to not bring the underworld fighters up until the battles had already begun.

Wanho didn't quite understand, but the demon had agreed reluctantly to wait while Kinaki spun his plans.

Today, though, wasn't about the coming war, not directly.

Unlike the other LandHolders, Kinaki had never felt the need to go on Promenade once he'd become LandHolder. As a young man he'd walked the borders at the behest of his father, along with his brothers, sisters, and many cousins. He recalled those times with fondness.

His own two children, along with their cousins, were currently on Promenade. Messengers had arrived the day before letting Kinaki know that the group would be arriving at the capital city of Jinyi that afternoon.

Kinaki was looking forward to talking with the group, listening to their impressions of the land, the border, and of the greatness that one of them was sure to inherit.

He remembered his own father talking about how much he learned from his children's Promenades. As LandHolder, Kinaki knew what was happening in the land in every corner of the House of Cobalt. The Promenades provided insight to the temperament of the people, what those far away from the court actually felt and thought.

Though most people were very careful around the powerful Holders, he still knew that some would slip up, that this group would have impressions that would be useful.

Of course the demon Wanho didn't see the point.

He was about to learn the importance of the everyday people.

❀

THE FEAST WELCOMING the travelers was long finished, and Kinaki's belly was still comfortably full. Wanho didn't insist on gluttony, just new and different tastes, spices, and textures. His cooks had taken it as a challenge to bring him a new dish to try at least once a week.

Kinaki and the group of travelers had moved from the grand dining hall to a cozier setting. Chairs and couches lined the walls, and a beautiful sunset shone just past the windows. Colorful pillows made every seat comfortable. Even in here, patterns of flowers were starting to make themselves known. Though Kinaki hadn't ever paid that much attention to the banners and tapestries draped on the walls, now he saw that flowers and lovely green vines had been added to the two hanging in the room, the colorful stitches overlaying what had been there.

Had the extra decorations been placed there by human hands? He didn't know, and he didn't want to know. Their presence (and that question) made him take another large gulp of his heavily spiced red wine, the warmth in his belly never quite taking away the chill that remained along his back. The smell of smoke increased for a moment. He looked at the small fire in the hearth, but saw no need for concern.

Chaotu, Kinaki's son, had become the *de facto* leader for the group, which Kinaki felt was only right. Chaotu was a thoughtful young man, in his late teens, sharp as a pickax and smarter than most. He had Kinaki's dark coloring, black hair, and soulful eyes, blended with his mother's pointed nose and chin.

Though Kinaki didn't know for certain who the land would choose to be his heir, he sincerely hoped that it would choose Chaotu and not Lijun, his daughter, who still had the fanaticism of youth. She'd been overly enamored of Belam and the Temple of Truth, and missed her old mentor.

Although, now that Wanho inhabited Kinaki's body, it would be quite a few years before anyone would inherit. Maybe Kinaki should marry off both Chaotu and Lijun early, so that they could start producing children, one of whom might become Kinaki's successor, someday far, far in the future.

After many stories and much laughter, the group quieted, a natural pause in the conversation. Kinaki prompted them, "What else do you have to tell me?"

As one, everyone looked to Chaotu. He grimaced and nodded, taking a swig of his wine before standing up. "LandHolder, we need to talk about the ghosts."

"Ghosts?" Kinaki asked, startled, though a thread of apprehension wormed its way into his belly. "What about the ghosts?"

"They've changed," Chaotu said. "First of all, there aren't as many of them as there once were."

"Nonsense," Kinaki said. "It is no longer ghost month. Of course there aren't as many now as there have been. They will come back as fall turns to winter, as they always do."

Chaotu stubbornly shook his head. "No," he said forcefully. "Even though it is not the month when ghosts are the most plentiful, there are still fewer than there should be."

"Who can control the ghosts?" Kinaki said, trying to dismiss the point.

But Chaotu went on. "The people are afraid. They think that their ancestors have abandoned them. That something so shameful has occurred that the dead no longer want anything to do with the living."

"How strange," Kinaki said. There really wasn't anything else he could say. He shrugged, trying to downplay Chaotu's point.

He'd become aware, though, that those from the underworld that Wanho had brought with him sometimes fed on the ghosts, then would steal all the smoke and offerings made to them. Wanho had assured Kinaki that it wouldn't be all the ghosts and that no one would notice a few missing.

How could he deflect the people's attention away from the ghosts? Maybe he could concoct a story that Sunli would believe, and get the priest to spread that explanation through all the Temples of Truth.

"The ghosts who remain, well, some of them are different," Chaotu said. He took another sip from his cup, as if he needed its warmth to bolster him.

Kinaki forced himself to smile when his son looked at him. He understood the implication. *He* was different, therefore the land, as well as its ghosts, were starting to reflect that.

"The ghosts are greedier," Chaotu said. "Demanding more sacrificial flame and smoke. More than one of the priests commented to us about how the ghosts have lost their white sheen and have taken on a red hue. The ghosts seem more powerful as well, able to move things in the physical world."

"What do you mean?" Kinaki said. He hadn't heard anything about that from Sunli. Then again, the head priest of the Temple of Truth was so concerned about the minutia of the temple, such as the colors of flowers being brought in as well as the cleanliness of the palace, that he may have stopped paying attention to the ghosts.

"Ghosts have always been able to make people feel cold,"

Chaotu said. He started to sound defensive. "But now, they heat things as well. Even start their own fires."

"I've heard many wild tales before, but I didn't expect such from you," Kinaki said, knowing that he sounded harsher than he'd intended when he saw his son flinch. "Who would have thought that you would take your seat in the marketplace and tell tales?"

Chaotu's eyes flashed with anger, then he took a breath and controlled himself.

Really, the boy was astonishingly well behaved. Despite the confrontation, Kinaki still felt admiration for his boy.

"I saw it myself," Chaotu said flatly. "The ghosts have changed."

The words rang out in the silent room, like a temple bell announcing the death of a major Holder.

"What do you expect me to do about it?" Kinaki said. "Even as LandHolder, I can't control the ghosts."

Chaotu looked around the room at his companions. They'd obviously all talked about this. In addition, at least Chaotu had expected this response from Kinaki.

Kinaki couldn't kill them all. Not outright. But some of these cousins might end up at the front of the battle lines with the CollierHolders.

He pushed the thought away. It wasn't worthy of the LandHolder.

But he was no longer merely a LandHolder, but the Holder of the House of Cobalt as well as the underworld.

"Then there are the auguries," Chaotu said.

That was news to Kinaki, though he nodded as if he already understood. "Go on," he said, at least trying to sound encouraging.

"I know that Sunli isn't conducting any at this point, blaming it on Belam, and how he overreached himself," Chaotu said. "But all the priests are having difficulty, even with the simplest divination. It's as if a barrier stands between them and the ghosts and ancestors who used to guide our way."

"I will have to look into this," Kinaki said. It had never occurred to him that when he'd given their ghosts to the demons that his house would lose one of its primary advantages—the ability to see the future, to know that their acts had the blessings of the gods as they'd been foretold.

He was surprised that he hadn't realized this lack in the House of Cobalt. Then again, Sunli had announced that the important events were being foretold on schedule, such as picking the most auspicious day for the start of the Promenade or where the miners should start digging next.

Surely someone was seeing the future clearly in order to direct such tasks.

"Anything else? More bad news?" Kinaki said.

Again, Chaotu looked around the room at the others.

Kinaki had the impression that they all warned him no, not to go ahead.

"Those are the most concerning ones, LandHolder," Chaotu said. "Thank you for giving us the opportunity to bring these points to your attention." He gave a stiff bow as though they were finishing an interview in front of the court.

"I appreciate you coming to me," Kinaki said, standing and giving a short bow in return. "I will consider these matters carefully." He wasn't about to promise that he could do anything. They had to understand that he didn't control the ghosts.

They all nodded, though the group seemed resigned. They left soon after that, claiming tiredness from the road and a great desire to go sleep in their own beds, something that Kinaki remembered well from his own Promenades.

It wasn't until much later that evening as Kinaki was

sliding into his own dark sleep that he realized how Chaotu had addressed him.

Not as Father, but as LandHolder.

Neither of his children ever called him Father anymore.

Surely it didn't matter. They were just growing up, and recognizing not only his place in the world, but theirs as potential heirs as well.

It still bothered him. The next day, though he didn't like giving the order, he insisted that Sunli set his spies to follow the group and report back on when they met next.

Chapter Fifteen
HOUSE OF GOLD

❧❧❧

Torja LOOKED at the clump of *fletche* in the middle of her telling cloth and despaired. She sat alone in her rooms, the lights from the magical lamps in the corners lowered due to her theory that maybe shadows cast by brighter illumination were somehow interfering with how the *fletche* fell.

Her rooms looked much softer now than when she'd first inherited them. Brightly embroidered pillows covered the hard stone window seat. Hunks of different colors of fabric hid the rock walls. Ribbons decorated the door frame as well as the edges of the windows. The quilt on her bed held as many outrageous, non-matching patterned cloth pieces that she could find, slowly sewing them on top of the much more formal and grand gold and silver that had been considered appropriate for someone at her level. Gauzy curtains hung from a ring above the bed, making her feel like a major Holder every time she climbed in.

She'd even draped a tiny cloth cloak woven in a pattern of rainbows across the shoulders of the small statue of the God Djediese who stood behind his altar in the corner.

But despite the warmth and colorfulness of the room,

Torja still felt a cold deep in her bowels, one that she hadn't been able to banish for months.

What good was it to be the head of the Temple of Truth if she had no ability to actually tell the truth of what was going to happen?

Ever since that fateful day more than a year before, Torja had encountered difficulty casting auguries and foretelling the future. She blamed it on the spirit of that slug who'd stolen away the *fletche* from her cloth. The Bandit SlugHolder who blocked even her puniest attempts at foretelling, who seemed so much mightier than the God Djediese and his attendants.

Of course, Torja's rivals still came up with the most perfect auguries. She'd had to rely on them more than once, humbling herself while swearing them to secrecy.

She had no idea how long before the news of her failure made itself known. Sooner or later, someone in the court would find out, and Torja would be removed as head of the Temple of Truth. She'd be driven into the street, with no place to call home.

Or worse, they'd banish her. Not just from the city, though. Make her live in lands outside of the House of Gold. They might even inflict the ultimate punishment, and send her into the barbarian lands, to live with those who had no sense of the land.

Torja sighed as she looked over her *fletche*. There was no pattern. No simple words that could be spelled out. No matter how many or how few of the pieces of wheat that she threw, they always ended up in a jumbled mess.

With a resigned sigh, Torja made herself get up off the floor. She'd tried kneeling on the cold hard stone more than once, but that hadn't given her a more successful augury, so she'd gone back to being comfortable and placing pillows down first.

She left the failed augury where it was. Maybe the *fletche* needed more time outside of their stuffy satchel, needed more air to breathe before they'd give her an augury.

In her heart of hearts, she knew that it didn't matter. Nothing she'd tried had worked. New *fletche*, new telling cloth, trying augury at all times during the day and night, in her rooms, in the temple, outside in the wind and cold or even blazing sunlight.

Every once in a while she would get some sort of foretelling. But never often or consistent enough that she felt she could figure out a pattern of what was wrong.

No one had strong enough magic to block an augury. That was just foolish. But sometimes she wondered about the Bandit SlugHolder who'd cast such a chill across the land…

Fortunately, or maybe not, Torja hadn't believed that she'd be able to cast an accurate augury that night and so hadn't bothered to change out of her formal robes into something more comfortable. She left her rooms and made her way across the base of the temple, hurrying to Ragna's rooms located at the back.

Torja often envied the other woman's rooms. They looked out over the back garden, a place that Torja loved. Except that Ragna didn't appear to appreciate the view, and kept her windows shuttered most of the time.

With a sigh, Torja knocked on Ragna's door. The other woman answered it instantly. Had she been waiting for Torja? Had she known that the head of the temple would be unable to cast yet another augury and would be relying on her for help?

"Good evening," Ragna said, bowing her head. She hung onto the door tightly as if afraid to open if further. She had the typical pale coloring of people from the House of Gold, her blonde hair hanging down in a long braid, her blue eyes still brilliant in the dim light. Her age was starting to show in the fine wrinkles gathered around the corners of her mouth, which constantly frowned in disapproval. She wore a beautifully decorated, long off-white shirt dress, with gold and green embroidery down the front along either side of the pearl buttons as well as across the front and shoulders.

"May I come in?" Torja said, puzzled by Ragna's stiffness.

Ragna opened her mouth then shut it again. She obviously wanted to refuse.

"Do you have a companion with you?" Torja asked, more curious than anything else. The priests and priestesses in the lands of the House of Gold were not required to take vows of celibacy, though she knew that some of her counterparts in the other lands did.

"No," Ragna said immediately, as if offended by the question.

Torja nearly snorted. She wasn't some delicate child who'd never seen or heard mating before. She had her own companions now and again, though never anyone that she'd wanted to marry.

Like most of the other temple priestesses, she was too busy to take the time for much companionship.

"Then what are you hiding?" Torja said. She expected another fierce denial, that Ragna wasn't hiding anything at all.

Instead, the other woman hung her head in shame and opened the door wider for Torja to enter.

Ragna's rooms were only slightly smaller than Torja's, but considerably more formal, the stiff rock not hidden by cloth. They were also colder, though rocks that could be heated were piled high in the fireplace between the windows.

In the middle of the sitting room, Ragna's telling cloth was spread out. Her *fletche* were cast in a jumble in the middle of it.

It took Torja a moment to figure out what she was

seeing. At first she thought that Ragna had merely dumped out her *fletche* from the satchel onto her cloth. Torja had done that before, when the *fletche* hadn't wanted to be drawn out of the bag and she'd up ended up holding the satchel and shaking it until all the *fletche* had fallen out.

But no. The bag was nowhere to be seen.

Ragna had been trying to cast an augury. And had been as successful as Torja had been.

"How long?" Torja said. Ragna flinched at Torja's tone. Good. "How long have you been having troubles casting auguries?"

Ragna kept her eyes firmly on the ground near her feet. "Since last year," she whispered. "Ever since you've been having difficulty."

Torja stayed where she was instead of marching over to Ragna and slapping the other priestess silly. How *dare* Ragna lie to her? Pretend that auguries were easy for her? That it was only Torja who was having trouble foretelling the future?

"And I'm assuming that the others are having the same problem?" Torja said.

Ragna nodded, miserable.

"Have you just been lying to me? Making up dates and names?" Torja said, still fuming. "Coming up with what seemed like the perfect solution, all by yourself? With no influence from the gods?"

"We had to!" Ragna said, finally looking up, her eyes blazing. "The Temple of Truth—we would have lost so much of our power! Our favor! No one would have listened to us, or to Unnir if we'd told the court the truth."

The reality of their predicament washed across Torja like a cold, hard wave.

Ragna was right. They couldn't tell Unnir or anyone else of their troubles. Or else they'd all be removed. Possibly banished. Though who would do the spell if it was the head of the Temple of Truth being banished?

Torja nodded finally. It felt to her as though her mind was racing through options and alternatives so quickly that she should start panting. "Do you have any idea why we can't foresee the future? Is what's coming so awful that we can't look ahead? Or is it something else?"

"I don't know," Ragna said, her anger fading. "It's as if the gods themselves have turned their backs on us."

Torja didn't roll her eyes at the other woman's overly dramatic proclamation. "No, that's not it."

While some thought that the gods gave them the auguries, Torja had never believed that, though she hadn't bothered debating the idea with anyone. She'd always thought that there was a closer intermediary who nudged the *fletche* this way or that. The gods couldn't be bothered to reach down and help them. That just didn't make sense to her.

"What are we going to do?" Ragna said, her despair evident.

"We keep lying," Torja said, though it hurt her to say it.

At Ragna's incredulous expression, Torja continued. "We need to keep the House of Gold stable. The Temple of Truth strong. We won't always have to lie. We will keep experimenting. I will set someone to researching ancient myths to find other ways to do divination. We will come through this."

Ragna's shocked look gave way to a soft smile. "You know, I never approved of you being promoted above me. I even blamed you at first for the troubles we were having with auguries. Now, though, I wonder if you were the right choice. I would have despaired long ago. All you do is keep fighting."

Torja shook her head and laughed, not bothering to

conceal the bitter note it contained. "My mother used to say that there was a fine line between stubborn and stupid and that I usually didn't even know which side I stood on." Then she took a deep breath. "We will continue," she said with a conviction she didn't actually feel. "We will determine the cause of our problems and we will overcome it."

With that, Torja swept out of Ragna's rooms, determined to find a way out of this predicament, the irony of the Temple of Truth needing to lie not lost to her.

It wasn't until Torja was back in her own, soft rooms with the door closed safely behind her that she sagged and let herself feel as lost as the little girl she'd been when her mother had first gotten sick. And though it had been many years since her mother had died, Torja still missed her.

Would her mother have any advice for her now? Or would she be ashamed of her daughter, lying instead of stepping down and letting someone else more capable take her place?

Torja didn't know. And though all the various Temples of Truth dealt with the ghosts and the dead, she didn't consider it her place to ask.

Instead, she started focusing on her current plans. She would toss a single *fletche* onto the telling cloth, as she had before, and spin lies from that.

It was better than nothing, or so she tried to convince herself all through the long, cold night.

Chapter Sixteen
HOUSE OF PEARL

❧

Shimokoro was not dismayed by his assistant's inability to get an accurate augury from even the special cave two days north of the palace. The anguish of his assistant's failure was palpable and remained in Shimokoro's office long after the assistant had left, as if it had seeped into the brick walls and stayed there, echoing faintly.

Fortunately, Shimokoro had been expecting this. Darikuto had warned of such an outcome, with the underworld demons sipping on the sacred smoke reserved for the ghosts and ancestors.

Plus, The Plan was so audacious that none could accurately predict its course. Shimokoro and his predecessor had provided only minor input to the formation of it. Certainly, they had had some visions which had helped. But Shimokoro had taken to using the pools merely as a spying glass on what was happening currently, not attempting to peek into the future.

And even then, the mirror wasn't always clear. He assumed that as more of The Plan came into being that his ability to see would lessen, and whatever visions did come would be less pristine.

So instead of worrying, Shimokoro sat in his office for a few more moments, relishing the quiet, trying to forget the hysteria of his associate. He was going to have to invite his assistant to retire, and soon. Yes, it wouldn't be difficult to convince the man that he'd lost his power and needed to go spend time with his son and grandchildren.

Who should be his replacement? Shimokoro thought about it, considering and rejecting names of acolytes. He understood the irony: This very important choice would now be made completely without augury. Maybe he should find someone younger, someone more malleable…

He put that thought to the side and pushed himself up and away from his deck. The office was comfortable enough for him. Not as austere as Chuyoko's rooms, but not overly decorated in black, silver, and pearls. Just a few touches to indicate Shimokoro's place in the LandHolder's household, such as the beautifully handbound leather volumes that lined the shelves to the right of his wide desk, the fine tile mosaic of waves and winds that covered the floor, and the pearl-encrusted black-and-silver suit of armor that stood on a fighting dummy in the corner, given to Shimokoro by the LandHolder himself.

There might come a time when Shimokoro would have to leave words aside and actually done the metal and leather suit. It wasn't heavy armor, but it would protect him from most injuries, particularly with the peaked silver helmet that sat proudly on the table next to the suit.

The demons would hopefully all stay in the House of Cobalt's lands and not cross over to the other houses. But Darikuto had plans in case they did.

Shimokoro wondered what plans the LandHolder had

for the major Holders who knew of The Plan, if they would all see the time of peace after the battles.

No matter if they did or didn't. Shimokoro was convinced that he would. He'd proven his worth to the LandHolder repeatedly.

Tonight, it was time to put into place yet another piece of bedrock that would cement Shimokoro's future.

Shimokoro slipped on a black wool cloak that had been hanging on a hook next to the door, drawing the hood over his head, then pausing a moment to cast a touch of magic.

He wasn't proficient with illusions. Anyone who knew him was likely to recognize him, as his height gave him away. Instead, Shimokoro placed a different type of glamour over himself, one that caused the eye to slide away. People wouldn't really notice him, or remember him, when he passed by. Not unless they were actively looking for him, like a messenger.

It wasn't a perfect disguise, but it was good enough for that evening.

Shimokoro slipped out of the palace using more modest hallways that he suspected none of his more important cohorts even knew about. The night outside was cool even this late in the summer, the stars hidden by low clouds and the magical lights that shone from every corner.

It was late enough that not many people remained on the broad wooden walks that lined the gravel streets. The buildings closest to the palace were stone and brick, giving way to wood as he passed out of the richer parts to the poorer and desperate.

No one truly went without in the lands of the House of Pearl. All were given succor, a place to sleep, and some sort of work to do. However, not everyone could be fully accommodated. There were widowers who had no skills, warriors who battled with drink, farmers who had left their holds to try their luck in the city. They had enough to survive on and not much else.

Those who came from such poor areas were frequently hungry for more. Too much magic abounded in the city for petty crimes, though. No one dared resort to robbery—such a thing would only end up with them hanging. Almost everyone had magical protection for their wallets, or could go to the Temple of Truth to ask who'd committed the crime and be told with accuracy.

Shimokoro didn't need an augury to foresee that there would be trouble as the ability to peer into the past as well as predict the future dwindled. He wasn't certain if all magic would lessen, but he suspected it might.

Hopefully, most of the misfits would find better wages and more thrills in the ranks of fighters. Plus, he knew that Chuyoko had plans to forcefully invite many of the poorer people to enlist, not really giving them any choice.

There would be many changes ahead, and not all of them would be welcome.

Finally, Shimokoro reached his destination, a tavern that served rice beer that was marginally better than swill, though they also had hearty stews that were acceptable and black bread that was considered tasty by many. The noise coming from the closed door, across the courtyard, made him pause for the first time that night. He'd expected most of the patrons to be seated at the tables outdoors, not inside.

Whatever was going on in there?

Then he heard cheers through the yelling.

Some sort of contest. Curious, Shimokoro pushed his way through the door, into the overheated room.

While the palace was made of brick and stone, the tavern showed its humbler beginnings, being made out of wood. Wood that appeared scorched by torches burning with true fire, instead of lighted magical stones. The smoke already gathered in the place made Shimokoro blink furiously for a moment until he got hold of his senses.

In the far corner opposite the door a group of people were playing darts. Most of the crowd were gathered around them, cheering and jeering, insulting the players as well as each other.

It surprised him to see a priest from the Temple of Truth standing beside the dartboard, his eyes closed, his hands held out just above his thighs, a position of deep concentration.

When the next throw didn't land spot in the middle of the bullseye, Shimokoro finally understood the priest's significance.

He was there to make sure that no one cheated, that they merely used physical abilities and not magic in order to direct their darts. He'd probably feel even the slightest whiff of magic so Shimokoro resolved not to get any closer to the game.

Luckily, he spotted his accomplice over in the corner, also sitting with his back to the wall, drinking.

As soon as Shimokoro grabbed himself a mug of beer, Benitoyo passed by while nodding to him, indicating that they should go outside to sit among the much quieter and cooler tables. Shimokoro followed, all too happy to leave the noise, the smoke, and the lights behind.

Benitoyo raised his own glass in a silent toast after Shimokoro sat down on the wooden bench that had been smoothed by the passing of many people over the years.

"What news do you bring?" Shimokoro asked quietly. Though he liked the merchant, he didn't want to be seen spending time talking with the man. He would much rather that everyone assumed Shimokoro got all of his news through magic and auguries, not through his complex network of spies.

Benitoyo pursed his full lips together for a moment

before he spoke. "Kinaki appears to have made a full recovery from whatever it was that we were feeding him." He held his hand up before Shimokoro could object. "Don't give me any guff about how it was harmless. I tried it myself." He gave an abrupt shiver and Shimokoro knew that he spoke the truth.

"But how Kinaki recovered…no one is completely sure. He appears different. Short tempered, much more so than before. His skin is redder than it used to be. He grows restless easily. He cannot sit for long periods of time. It's been whispered that snakes now live in his body, and can be seen sliding across his torso, underneath his robes."

Shimokoro merely nodded. He wasn't about to illuminate Benitoyo as to the true condition of the LandHolder.

"Sickeningly sweet flowers dominate every room of the palace," Benitoyo said. He took a sip of his beer, as if clearing away the floral taste. "No one knows why. Patterns of flowers and vines have shown up in all the tapestries as if sewn there, but no one has touched those hangings for years." He paused, nodding as if going over points in his head.

"Though Sunli and the Temple of Truth are trying to deny it, augury has become much more difficult," Benitoyo continued.

Shimokoro kept a pleasant enough smile on his face rather than nod as well. He was well aware of those issues. He'd actually heard most of this before.

"The children of the Hold have come back from their Promenade with reports of the same, spread throughout the land," Benitoyo continued. "The ghosts have changed. Gotten greedy, as well as stronger." He looked over the top of his beer at Shimokoro, as if trying to see what the other man thought of such a thing.

Shimokoro said, "Go on." He was curious about what effect the demons were having on the House of Cobalt.

Benitoyo shrugged. "I've never been much for dealing with ghosts or looking toward the past. The future can change with a single draw of the cards, you know? But those that rely on them no longer can. The people are restless. I keep Sunli distracted as well as I can."

"Good," Shimokoro said. "Now, what can you tell me of Kinaki's troops?"

Benitoyo gave a feral grin at that. "Officially, all those warriors have been gathered to fight off the barbarians coming at the land from the south. Except that many don't ever see any battles, or even barbarians. Instead, they train and fight and gain experience with each other, going through choreographed combat and sparring matches."

"How many?"

"He's amassed at least fifty thousand," Benitoyo said. At Shimokoro's surprised blink, Benitoyo replied, "Someone has to supply all those warriors with weapons, armor, and food. Of course, I don't have all the contracts, though I do control the majority of them through sub-contractors. Merchants who cannot be traced back to me."

"Most excellent," Shimokoro said. This was the information he really needed—an accurate account of what Chuyoko and the other PearlHolders would be facing. It was yet another way for Shimokoro to prove his worth to Darikuto, by feeding the LandHolder information like this.

Benitoyo continued to give Shimokoro details about the exact location of the warriors as well a guess as to how many were in each camp. He didn't know their orders or what they were doing—he didn't have any spies in with the troops. He could only extrapolate things from the supplies he delivered.

"Good, good," Shimokoro said. He knew that he needed to move along, before anyone actually noticed the pair of them talking, even though it was nighttime and they were outside, not in the crowded tavern. "I need one more thing from you. Tell me about the security of the palace of the House of Cobalt itself. The guards there."

Benitoyo hesitated.

"The information will never be traced back to you," Shimokoro assured the merchant. "It will all come from blessed augury."

The huge grin that greeted those words surprised Shimokoro. "That's what I thought," Benitoyo said. "All the lands will have difficulty with augury, won't they? Until whatever happened to Kinaki is set to right."

Shimokoro shrugged. "I don't know what you're talking about."

Benitoyo gave a hearty laugh and drained his mug of beer. Then he passed along all the information that Shimokoro could ever want about the security of the House of Cobalt in the palace, how often the guards changed, their routes, the easiest ways into and out of the main building and the surrounding area.

"Not that I've ever tried any of those routes myself," Benitoyo finished with a broad wink.

"The LandHolder will be pleased with everything you've told us," Shimokoro said as he finished his own beer that had grown flat as it had warmed.

"That's good," Benitoyo said. "I am counting on my own Hold when this business is over."

"Of course!" Shimokoro said immediately, though he had never made any such plans for Benitoyo.

The merchant would have outlived his usefulness once the wars started in earnest.

Benitoyo gave the priest an easy smile. "Good. There are letters already in the hands of my heirs detailing our bargain. As well as clear scripts of what should be said if I should die suddenly or suspiciously while in foreign lands."

Shimokoro didn't insult the man by looking shocked that he wasn't trusted. "I see," he said. "You do realize that there will be casualties in the coming war."

Benitoyo nodded. "Yes. And I may accidentally be one of them. As long as it's really the fortune of war and not the deliberate interference of priests, my heirs will be satisfied."

"There won't be any way of verifying, you know," Shimokoro warned.

"I'll know what happened," Benitoyo insisted. "And I will endeavor to make sure that my heirs know as well."

Shimokoro wasn't certain what that meant, or how Benitoyo would be able to ensure that. However, he took the merchant at his word.

It just meant that more of the House of Pearl's people would die when the war started. Benitoyo's family, for instance.

Such were the casualties of The Plan.

Chapter Seventeen
HOUSE OF CRYSTAL

❦

HAPTOMI OPENED his eyes and glared at the perfectly innocent crystals that sat in a bowl before him on his desk.

No matter what he did, the crystals stayed the same. They didn't glow. They didn't emit warmth or chilled air. No visions rose from them like a dream. They didn't speak in any language known to man.

They were inert, like salted earth.

Haptomi shifted uncomfortably in his chair, uncertain of what to do next. The incense beside the bowl still smoldered, a thin trail of smoke rising to the ceiling of his office. Though he'd always enjoyed the floral scent, it now made him uneasy, maybe because he'd failed (again!) to have a vision.

He reached out and ran a finger along the edge of the bowl. It was made from the finest polished silver that his personal attendant kept well-polished. The lump of crystal sitting in the center of the bowl had a dark purple base that fit comfortably into the palm of his hand. An irregular formation of clear spikes jutted out from that into the air, maybe six inches tall.

Haptomi had tried different crystals, different

configurations. He'd even tried sitting on the floor like a barbarian (though he had used a cushion).

Nothing had worked. His ability to cast auguries, to catch visions from the crystals, had diminished tremendously over the past year. It had appeared that the God Djediese had turned his back on them.

Haptomi would have stepped down from his position as head of the Temple of Truth if no one else had lost their ability. Yet, as far as he knew, all magical abilities were slowly draining out of the lands of the House of Crystal.

Why? No one knew.

The Chamber of Crystals at least still responded to him. Every time he walked down those dark, narrow stairs, he worried that this would be the time that no lights would greet him. Yet, every time, the chamber lit up like a holiday party.

Of course, the chamber no longer answered any questions. It still welcomed him like an old friend. It was as if the Chamber of Crystals had grown into an ancient, poor relation, someone who would turn up all the lights when you came to visit, but would never offer you any food or wine.

Haptomi stubbornly went to see the chamber once every ten days, regardless of whether it answered questions or not. It was probably his imagination that it grew lonely between his visits.

Ibitsima also continued to send her children to the chamber regularly. Haptomi tried not to feel too much pride in the fact that the Chamber of Crystals rarely lit up for them anymore.

And then there was Akalina.

Haptomi sat back in his chair, drumming his fingers on his desk as he contemplated the mystery of the girl.

She'd grown this last year, becoming tall and willowy. Her black hair fell like a cloud around her face. Even when she kept it pinned back it was always escaping and standing out around her head like a wispy mane. It made her white skin more prominent, and her wide eyes rounder. She was always so quiet, startling Haptomi more than once when she spoke or moved.

It was as if she were part ghost.

The chamber appeared to be split in its opinion about her. Sometimes when she approached, it would light up like it did for Haptomi.

Frequently, however, it remained spitefully black. Eerie, freezing winds appeared out of nowhere and blew around her, carrying the scent of limestone and old bones.

Was she the next LandHolder? Haptomi would have bet on it before.

Now, he was unsure.

Ever since Rosahaptu had touched the girl, the ghosts had diminished. This year, the court of the ghosts was frequently empty. It was unheard of.

The land itself was unsettled as well. He could tell from how restless the LandHolder was, how difficult it was for her to sit in one place for very long.

Fortunately, in three weeks' time, they'd make the long trip across the lands of the House of Gold and head to the House of Cobalt for the annual gathering of the LandHolders.

The festival was always held at the end of the summer, when the majority of the crops had been harvested and the markets were full to bursting. Haptomi approved of this, knowing that it was a ploy by the LandHolders to brag about the bounty of their land.

The House of Crystal was in subdued uproar at the moment as they packed and planned and Ibitsima made choices about who should travel with them and who should not.

Haptomi aided her when he could, providing seasoned advice when he found he couldn't rely on augury or the crystals. He was certain the LandHolder appreciated all of his opinions.

There was one point on which they couldn't agree, however.

Should Akalina go with the household to the House of Cobalt?

The girl hadn't done anything wrong. However, she'd turned seventeen that spring and still had yet to start her menses. As far as the LandHolder could tell, the girl wasn't sick or anything.

The land would never choose a barren LandHolder, either male or female. Haptomi knew of no legend when that had occurred. The LandHolder had to be able to procreate, to create potential heirs.

Would Akalina start her menses before the household left? Or would she be left behind?

Haptomi didn't know, and no augury would show him the truth.

As the head of the Temple of Truth, he had the right to accompany the LandHolder. It would be a good time for him to catch up with the other leaders of the temples. He really wanted to talk with them, to find out if everyone was having as much difficulty with divination.

Ibitsima said they were, at least according to her spies.

Haptomi didn't have his own spy network. He'd never had to do anything as distasteful as that. He had certainly never approved of Ibitsima's spies, believing that she should trust the crystals instead.

It appeared her method may have been more prudent in the long run.

But her spies couldn't answer the one question he had, the one which no augury would be able to tell him.

Was Akalina to be the next LandHolder? He knew that she was important. It was a tickling sensation that he couldn't deny, even if he tried. The notion wouldn't let him go. She'd been *Chosen*. He was certain of it.

But chosen to do what?

With a sigh, Haptomi pushed himself back from his desk, leaving his neat, clean office and walking into the quiet chaos of the palace, going to his appointment with the LandHolder. He wasn't looking forward to telling her of his latest failures. But he was determined to maintain the illusion that the Temple of Truth still could tell the truth.

Even if it was a mundane and ugly one.

Chapter Eighteen
HOUSE OF COBALT

❦

BENITOYO SAT in his well-appointed study. The fireplace held warm glowing rocks that kept off the chill of the night. Jinyi, the capital city of the lands of the House of Cobalt, was always so dry. He welcomed the moisture that caressed his skin when he returned home to the House of Pearl, to Yawatan, the capital.

And while he would have appreciated a real wood fire, and the heat that would sink into his bones, he knew that he didn't have the patience to keep tending it all through the evening. Not with the various meetings that he'd had with his now-adult children. Plus, he hadn't wanted any servants around that evening. So the magical rocks would have to provide enough warmth, though to his admittedly older bones, now that he was in his fifties, they weren't as effective.

He sat in a comfortable chair, not ostentatious but still padded to hold his weight, the back high enough that he could rest his head against it, as he did then. The crystal snifter on the table beside him was empty of the fine brandy it had held earlier, the warmth of the alcohol infusing his belly now. The shelves that lined the walls of the small room were filled not only with books but with knickknacks he'd picked up on his travels. A small altar to the God Xiuma sat in the corner, formed out of rich blue cobalt. He sat fat and happy on his throne, laughing. Piles of gold coins and precious stones were strewn around his feet. Merchants and miners all prayed to him for good fortune.

Over the fireplace hung a beautiful oil painting of Benitoyo and his entire family when the children had been nine, seven, and five, done well over a decade ago. His wife Ozukshi outshone everyone, of course.

As if the thought had summoned her, his wife came gliding into the room. He always marveled at how graceful she was in everything that she did—walking, singing, dancing, organizing the household, making love.

She carried another glass of brandy with her, anticipating his needs. She placed it on the table beside him with a knowing smile, picking up the empty glass. She paused, looking at him.

"You look tired," she said softly. "You should go to bed soon."

"Only if you will come with me to warm the sheets," Benitoyo said gamely.

"Of course," Ozukshi said.

He took her hand in his but remained seated, looking up at her. She wore a plain robe, made of fine linen tinted the color of pale gold, with a beautiful design of red poppies woven into it. It suited her, showing off her dark skin. The wide green belt at the waist gave her more of a figure, hugging her womanly hips. Her hair was cut shorter than most, as short as a man's. She'd always claimed that she didn't want to bother with it, though Benitoyo suspected she kept it so short because it made her even more striking and memorable. Her hand was small in his, with a brown palm and rough skin. She worked too hard, frequently doing tasks that were better suited for servants.

Not that Benitoyo ever chided her for it. She'd been raised as the daughter of a fisherman, not the head of a rich household. No one would ever be able to tell that by looking at her. It was really only her hands that gave her away.

She was still the most beautiful woman he'd ever seen. One of the smartest as well. She'd been the one who'd urged him to take Shimokoro's patronage, understanding that Benitoyo would no longer be just a merchant but a spy for the LandHolder.

It was a dangerous position. Benitoyo suspected that his wife enjoyed the potential thrill and risk of it more than he did. Then again, she'd been raised on the sea, and still stood outside when the storms came, welcoming the wild winds and slashing rain.

She was truly a child of the Goddess Morta, the goddess of the moon, who not only calmed the waters but brought the storms. Morta was also the goddess of the warriors, and although Ozukshi had never wielded a sword, with her words and her wit she was far from defenseless.

"What is it, my love?" Ozukshi said when Benitoyo continued to sit there and just look at her.

He tugged at her hand. She rolled her eyes at him but complied, curling up neatly in his lap like a house cat.

He draped his arms around her. Ah, this was the warmth that had been missing all night. He dropped his head closer to her so he could take in her spicy scent. He felt his manhood stir just with that faint whiff.

Yes, she still did that to him, even after all these years.

"The Plan continues unabated," he said softly. "The children know the parts they are to play."

He'd given them all enough pieces of the puzzle that they'd have to work together in order to avenge him if it came to that. Assuming they all lived through the coming war.

Only Ozukshi knew of his entire ambition—to blackmail Shimokoro into granting him a major Hold. He'd have to be able to hang on to it, would have to develop the landsense necessary for a large plot of land.

Or his children would have to. He'd made them practice their landsense and their magic ever since they'd been small, waiting for this type of opportunity.

It had been Ozukshi who'd advised him to try some of the powders that Benitoyo had been slipping into Kinaki's meals. His rooms were right across from the kitchen, so it had been easy to gain access to the salt that had been reserved for Kinaki.

Those powders had stolen all of his sense of the land. It had been like walking on ashes. He assumed that it had been worse for him than it had been for Kinaki as he'd taken a single large dose instead of a tiny amount over weeks and months.

Had great snakes risen from the ground to aid the LandHolder? Kinaki no longer wore tight clothing, but instead, loose robes that flowed from his great shoulders down to the floor, sleeves that billowed from shoulders to wrist, with tight cuffs, as if preventing anything from escaping down his arms.

Even with that, Benitoyo had thought he'd caught something gliding under Kinaki's robes once, like a muscle rippling across his chest.

A muscle three inches wide and round that slid from one shoulder to the other.

"Something else bothers you this evening," Ozukshi said. "What is it?"

Benitoyo sighed and hugged his wife closer. "Our fortunes will be greatly increased by the spying I've done," he said. He never lied to himself about what Shimokoro asked him to do, never hid the truth from his wife, either. "By how I poisoned the LandHolder of the House of Cobalt. But at what cost?"

He'd told her already how the land in the House of Cobalt was changing. Weird vines hung from trees, making the forests dark and muggy. Stinky flowers erupted from cracks between the rocks. Clouds of angry gnats pursued travelers, and constant magical vigilance had to be maintained or a person (and their livestock) would be eaten alive.

Ozukshi shrugged, an interesting, distracting experience given how tightly her body was pressed against his.

"There will be war," she said softly. "Lives will be lost. Darikuto has always had his plans, as did his father before him. The deaths have already been foretold in the great halls of the gods, their names placed on the lists of those accepted to the Golden Lands. If you hadn't helped The Plan along, someone else would have. Isn't it better that we have the chance to enrich ourselves and our family, make not only our children's lives better but their children's as well? There is nothing we could have done to stop Darikuto." She shrugged again. "Better to make the best of what we were handed."

Benitoyo sighed and nodded. He didn't have the strong faith that his wife did. Augury was never absolute. Otherwise, why live? Why stride? Why try to better yourself?

There really was no answer to his question. Ozukshi was right. They'd been presented with an opportunity and he'd grabbed it gleefully. Now was not the time for regrets.

"You're correct, of course," he said softly, kissing her neck.

Ozukshi caressed his jaw, then turned his head up so their lips met. More warmth flooded into Benitoyo, filling his belly and beyond.

"Sometimes actions are the only answer," Ozukshi said, resting her forehead against his, still caressing his face. "Let's go act together."

Benitoyo kissed her again, just because he could, then gladly took her to bed, delighting in her soft skin, her firm arms, how well they fit together, and how she made his entire world explode.

Afterward, spooning behind her as he dropped off to sleep, Benitoyo told himself yet again that there was nothing to worry about. Even if he was killed, his family would still be better off.

And the land? It would heal. It always did.

Chapter Nineteen

HOUSE OF GOLD

❦

UNNIR PACED her rooms late that night, alone and furious. She'd sent her husband off to his own quarters, knowing that she needed time by herself that evening while she put together all the reports that she'd heard that day, that week, by the great tombs, that year.

Yudur, the previous LandHolder, had quite an impressive network of spies. At first, Unnir hadn't known what to think of it. Did she really need to know what was happening in the other houses? Why did she need reports on not only the major Holders in the House of Gold, but the MinersHold as well as the GuildHold?

Though listening to all those reports took time, Unnir had left the networks in place. She'd not directed the spies at first, but instead, had just listened and absorbed all the information they gave to her. It was a constant trickle of facts that she could use to gauge what some of those same people said directly to her face.

It was only since that spring that she'd actually given any of her spies direct tasks. This time, namely, to spy on her cousins Emir and Vide. She was certain that they'd been agitating her warriors, the VeinHolders and their cohorts.

What she'd learned that evening though had sent a chill through her bones, as well as infuriated her.

It turned out that her cousins had been responsible for the great embarrassment that had happened the previous year, when the House of Gold had hosted the other LandHolders. They'd bribed merchants to not show up at the markets, or to come with poorer goods, so that it appeared that her lands were less bountiful than they actually were.

Unnir and her household were to leave for this year's gathering at the House of Cobalt in a few days. It seemed that her cousins were planning much more dire things this time.

How dare they think that they could sabotage her retinue? Breaking axles on carriages and spreading disease? Possibly poisoning the other LandHolders when it was her turn to host them all for an evening?

It was not to be tolerated.

But what could she do? She didn't really have any proof, just the words of spies. Unnir knew that she could ask Torja to test the accuracy of what she had learned, but was reluctant to draw in the Temple of Truth.

Though Unnir still felt every inch of her land, she knew that the magic was weakening. Auguries weren't as accurate. Miners weren't finding veins that they used to. The fields were still bountiful, but that was it. There were even fewer ghosts to plague the living than there had been.

Unnir debated demanding that her cousins come to her, to her chambers. She looked around the rooms. She'd deliberately softened the hard edges that Yudur had added. The rooms were decidedly feminine now. They were also her sanctuary, away from the rest of the court and the problems of her day.

No. She would go to them. It might make her appear weaker in their eyes, but they had no idea what a LandHolder could actually do, particularly once they'd made her angry.

❦

UNNIR BURST into Emil's door like a hot wind. She hadn't bothered knocking. She'd used a servant to verify that they were in there, together.

They sat at the far end of the front room, on either side of a fireplace that glowed with magically warmed rocks. They both drank her finest wine from goblets that probably belonged in her personal cupboards.

Emil wore a long-sleeved white shirt with ruffles around the cuffs and neck. His blond hair hung over one blue eye and he had a sullen look that he probably thought made him look romantic, like a wounded hero. Instead, he looked like a spoiled brat who expected everyone to leap to his bidding.

Vide was just as bad, though his coloring was darker and his eyes were a tawny color. His lips were twisted in a permanent smirk that she wanted to slap off of his face.

"Cousin," Emil said, starting to rise. "What can we do for you?"

"Sit," Unnir ordered, pointing at him.

A brief look of worry crossed his face before he blandly smiled at her. "Of course."

Unnir stared at the pair of them, letting the silence grow uncomfortable. Finally, she nodded, as if she'd just come to a decision when really, she knew what she wanted all along.

"First of all, you are to address me with my proper title. LandHolder," she said.

She didn't like the look that the pair of them exchanged, as if they weren't sure what she meant.

"I am the LandHolder for the House of Gold," she added.

"Of course you are," Vide said smoothly. "We know that."

"Then why the in the names of the Great Tombs haven't you been treating me that way?" Unnir fumed.

The cousins sat in shocked silence for a few moments as if they'd never expected her to confront them this way.

Good.

"I know of the little games you played last year, with the merchants and the farmers," Unnir said hotly. "How you bribed some of them to not bring their best goods to the markets, so that it appeared that the House of Gold under my management was no longer bountiful."

"I have no idea—" Vide started.

"Silence," Unnir said, "or I will silence you."

Emil shot a very worried look toward Vide. Vide stared hard at Unnir, his expression growing cold.

"Of course. LandHolder," Vide said very deliberately. It sounded so much like a sneer that Unnir did what she'd threatened to do.

A piece of wood detached itself from the tall back of the chair and whipped across Vide's mouth like a gag.

His eyes stared wide and shocked at her. She added restraints so that he couldn't move, his wrists and ankles now bound to the chair.

At least she'd managed to wipe that smirk from his face.

Then she turned to face Emil, who stared at her with his mouth open. Though he hadn't offered any offense, not like Vide, she gave Emil the same treatment, so that they now both sat bound and gagged in front of her.

She paced for a few moments, unsure of what to do next. But she had no questions of them. Had no doubt of their guilt no matter what source had brought it to her, or how much she'd had to pay for the truth.

"Now. You will both *immediately* stop these little games of yours. Stop tearing me down behind my back. Stop agitating the VeinHolders. Stop spreading lies about me to the FarmHolders. And you will *not* attempt to poison the other LandHolders when I host a feast at the gathering in two weeks' time!"

That was the part of their plan that really made her angry. The rocks in the fireplace responded to her rage, belching heat into the room. The walls started to shimmer, the air growing thick. The smell of baked stone filled the air.

Both cousins now looked frightened. As they should. It would be completely within her right to kill them both, right now, then present her evidence to the court.

It might actually bring her respect from some quarters. But she didn't want to earn it that way.

"Do you hear me?" Unnir said. When they didn't nod immediately, she stomped her foot.

The floor rolled, as if a wave had just passed under it. Brick walls creaked and shook with alarm. The loud crack of the hearthstones echoed through the room. Dust filled the air.

"Do you hear me?" Unnir asked again, her tone low and angry and unfamiliar.

This time both Emil and Vide nodded frantically.

"If I *ever* find out that you have gone behind my back to weaken my position again, I will slay you both, in front of all the Holders. I won't make it fast, either. I will tie you down and flay your skin from you first, letting your blood feed the earth. I will pierce your eyes with thorns so that you won't be able to see what's coming next. I will leave your mouths open so that your screams will act as warnings to everyone who has been under your sway. Have I made myself clear?"

Emil and Vide nodded more.

"We need to work together as a family," Unnir told them in a softer voice, her anger finally draining away. "If not, the threats we face will tear the entire House of Gold apart, and we will lose our lands. You won't just oust me. You'll oust our house as well."

They had no idea of the threats she faced, the niggling jabs from the other LandHolders, how much she needed them and their support.

But she would do it without them if she had to.

"I will not warn you a second time," she told them firmly. "I will simply slay you instead."

With that, Unnir turned and stomped out of Emil's rooms, removing her restraints only as she passed through the door.

More than one servant stood in the hallway agog. It seemed that Unnir in her anger had damaged the palace. Walls were cracked and tilted. Her rage had caused a small earthquake, centered in her cousin's rooms.

Damn it! She already knew that some of the gossips in the court would start agitating that she be removed, that she was uncontrollable and had let her anger get the best of her this way.

It didn't matter. She would rule them all, command their obedience if not their respect.

In the meantime, she would have to repair the damage she'd done, running her hands over the walls, closing the cracks and repairing the floors.

It was the least she could do.

Chapter Twenty
HOUSE OF PEARL

❧❧❧

DARIKUTO HAD MADE a Promenade early that spring. Unlike the other LandHolders, he traveled alone and used his magic to move him quickly from one end of his land to the other, traveling the entire distance in merely a week instead of more than six. Yawatan, the capital, was close to the center of the land in terms of north to south. However, the city was far to the west, located on a natural pier overlooking the ocean. He'd traveled down along the coast to the very southern tip, enjoying being so near the ocean, gathering the hard rocks and sand into his bone.

Then he'd traveled inland across the shifting lands. So many creeks and waterways ran through the earth that the marshy land itself was not stable. Instead, the people lived on houseboats, farming wetlands for rice and eating freshwater reeds and grains.

The northward route skirted the hills to the east, the demarcation between the House of Pearl and the other three houses. He spent one night on the highest hill looking toward the lands of the House of Cobalt. Hot winds greeted him, carrying the scent of decay, as if the summer had already passed and all the fields lay fallow and rotting.

The House of Gold lands, though they were between the House of Cobalt and the House of Crystal and generally temperate, always struck him as cold. Those people had more formality than any of the others, always concerned more with appearance than anything else. The LandHolder's cousins were dissatisfied with Unnir, and some of the gold they spent to cause trouble had been multiplied with coins from the House of Pearl.

Not that the cousins knew anything about that.

The lands of the House of Crystal, though physically the coldest, always seemed the warmest to him, reaching out with his landsense. Not the unhealthy heat of decay, but the glow of health. Ibitsima had recovered from the poison that Darikuto had tried giving her, unable to follow the same route that had worked for Kinaki. He felt closest to these lands. They were the most similar to his, despite how different the terrain was.

He would take them first.

Finally, Darikuto turned his face back toward the west, heading down to the ocean, then making his way along the coast back to Yawatan. He skimmed over the land like a stone over water, the days passing as if in a dream.

When Darikuto returned to the city, closing the rough rectangle, he felt renewed. Every corner and inch of his land was firmly in his grasp. He felt the tremendous power the territory gave him. He slept well that first night back in the palace and was more energized the following weeks and months.

That sense of energy had followed him, even across the border into the lands of the House of Cobalt.

Tomorrow, they would leave the foothills that divided Darikuto's land from Kinaki's, then spend a few days crossing the plains before they reached the city of Jinyi, just in time for the gathering of LandHolders.

It certainly would be one to remember.

Tonight, Darikuto stood outside his tent, facing east instead of west, across the dark lands. The hot winds had increased with every step they'd traveled toward Jinyi. The stench had increased as well. Over the last day, Darikuto had discovered why.

Brilliant yellow skunk cabbage bloomed out of season in whatever shade it could find, as rank as rotting meat. Large white flowers hung from thick vines between the trees— corpse bells, so called because of the putrid smell. Odd grasses with tall, sharp spikes at the ends grew like fence posts, or easy-to-harvest spears. They had a gassy smell, as if they'd originated in a fetid swamp.

Darikuto had to admit the change in the land of the House of Cobalt made him uneasy. He'd gone into the territory of the other LandHolders before, traveled to their houses. While there had always been some level of discomfort walking across land that wasn't his, he still recognized that land. It was akin to his own, even though it bore another's name. He could easily see possessing it.

The lands of the House of Cobalt had turned strange. It was as if a fire ran just under the surface, seething and angry, wanting to consume the souls of all those who walked above ground.

How much effort would it take to reclaim this land once the demons were exiled back to the underworld? Would the stinky flowers melt with the spring rains? Or would the LandHolder have to plow all the remnants of the demon possession under purified earth?

At least he wouldn't have to argue with the other LandHolders about Kinaki. They would all know that something was wrong. They wouldn't understand the depth of it, not until something happened. In the meantime, he would downplay their fears. He didn't want a confrontation.

Not yet.

Chuyoko and her warriors had their assignments. Shimokoro had been able to provide Darikuto with accurate floorplans of the palace, as well as information about the guards.

Darikuto didn't know which warrior would actually carry out the final deed. He didn't need to know. He knew that the Goddess Morta would bless and keep that warrior close to her bosom, despite the subterfuge.

The Plan would raise them all up, guarantee them all a spot in the Golden Lands.

The key was to keep them all distracted from the truth. Everyone would place the blame on Kinaki, never looking at Darikuto. No one could learn of The Plan until it was far too late, and even then they would still have to bow to the inevitable.

Perhaps by this time next year the battles would be over and there would be peace across the land, as well as a single LandHolder. He doubted that things would go that smoothly, though. However, now was not the time to become impatient. It would take more than a year to claim everything that was rightfully his. There would be disgruntled warriors, as well as Holders who would have to be dealt with, small rebellions.

And the land in front of him…this land would have to heal.

Of course, it would all work out in his favor at the end. No matter what the cost.

Chapter Twenty-One
HOUSE OF CRYSTAL

AKALINA SAT on the edge of her bed. The knife she held was small, shorter than the palm of her hand. The milky white crystal that had been smoothed over the handle warmed quickly to the touch. The sharp silver blade almost looked innocent nestled between her fingers.

She had set the lights in her room to a dim glow, needing to see but not wanting to see too clearly. She wore a white nightgown that covered her completely despite the heat of the banked rocks in the fireplace. Her bed was small, still a child's bed, narrow and hard.

Tomorrow, Ibitsima and the others would start their journey to the House of Cobalt. Ibitsima had pushed their departure date off to the very last minute. She would use her magic to move the group quickly across the lands so that they'd arrive on time, and only have to spend a minimum number of days away from home.

Part of the reason Ibitsima had delayed was for Akalina.

She was seventeen now. It was unheard of for a woman to start her menses this late.

If Akalina didn't bleed tonight, she would be left behind.

Haptomi had been very reluctant to deliver her the news. He'd been the one who'd assumed that she was the next LandHolder, who had been pushing Ibitsima to train her as she would her own children.

All of that privilege would disappear tomorrow if Akalina didn't start her period that night. Her own parents had also made it clear that they would want nothing to do with her if they couldn't use her marriage to make a strategic alliance.

Hence, the knife.

She just had to cut herself, just a little, down there inside of herself. It wouldn't take much. She'd have to do it every month to keep her place in the LandHolder's household.

Was it worth it?

The Temple of Truth wouldn't know of her deception. Not while they were having such difficulty with auguries. All magic was much harder to use. Simple tasks like lighting candles were now done with firesticks. Parts of the palace were cold and dark because no one could maintain the lighted and heated stones constantly. Farmers complained bitterly about bugs eating their crops as well as their animals. Merchants had problems maintaining the freshness of their goods.

The whole world had grown savage, as if the land itself was turning against them.

More altars had shown up in the city, dedicated to all four of the gods. Incense and fires were constantly lit under them. People had always paid attention to their ghosts—they had to, or the ghosts would cause mischief. Now, the ghosts had vanished, and people even prayed to get them to return.

Only Akalina saw the ghosts who still haunted the land. They acted scared, hiding in corners, as if they didn't want anyone to notice them. The white glow that had always filled them had been toned down. She caught them surreptitiously sipping at smoke instead of boldly demanding their share.

None of them attended the court of the ghosts.

Even Ibitsima couldn't counter whatever had frightened the ghosts.

Akalina longed to leave with everyone else. To proudly show her bloodied nightgown in the morning to her nurse. To still be part of the LandHolder's inner family.

The shame…the shame of being left behind made her shiver. It was an awful feeling, as if she were dirty somehow, her core unclean, unhealthy.

Maybe it was, since Rosahaptu had touched her.

No one in the court would want to deal with Akalina after this. In her worst nightmares, the LandHolder would banish her for being barren and for not being able to fulfill her duty to the household. Haptomi would strip away all her landsense.

Maybe she could become a priestess after all. Those in the temples for the House of Crystal never married. They rarely took companions either, instead dedicating themselves to their temple.

It would be a lonely existence. She might not have a choice, though.

Live her life as a lie? Or live her life alone?

She had to decide. That night. And quickly.

Akalina brought the blade to her lips, kissing the cool, smooth tip. It wouldn't take much. Just a prick. She drew her nightgown up around her waist, parted her legs, and nestled the knife down there. The blade pricked her skin softly. She urged her hand to move. Just a little. Upwards. Inwards.

The blade seemed heated against her skin. Was it yearning like a lover for her? To kiss her intimately?

Her hand started shaking. She wrapped her fingers more tightly around the hilt of the blade. Sweat built on her neck under her heavy braid of hair. The dim lights of the room swam. Akalina felt light-headed.

She just had to do this. One little prick. Keep her place. No one would know, or would discover the deceit, not until the LandHolder died and Akalina was not chosen. That would be so many years in the future a little cut now would seem like nothing.

It wasn't nothing, though. Her entire life would be built around a lie. Whoever married her would be deceived as well, not just one life but two ruined.

Please. Just a little cut.

Akalina couldn't make herself do it.

Trembling, she put the knife down on the table beside her bed. The blade pointed at her, like an accusing finger.

She'd had her chance. But she'd chosen the coward's way out, at least that was how some would see it. She'd refused to hurt herself, to dance with the blade and mar her skin to keep her position.

But she couldn't live a lie. That much she knew.

Akalina slept surprisingly well, and said goodbye to the household in the morning with dry eyes.

When they returned in three weeks' time, everything would change. For now, she lived in limbo.

Like a ghost.

Chapter Twenty-Two
HOUSE OF COBALT

Sunli could not believe what he was seeing! The flowers in the pots that lined the grand entranceway that all the LandHolders were to walk along were all wrong! There should have been bluebells, forget-me-nots, cornflowers, and violets. Every blossom should have been some shade of blue!

Instead, vines with white blossoms crept between the pots, as if trying to make walls on either side of the walkway. They smelled awful. Weird green and black flowers waved from the sides with petals that looked more like mis-colored leaves than proper blossoms. And the yellow flowers were so very, very wrong, like calla lilies that had grown under a weight, so the petals spread like a hand with an obscene-looking spike sticking straight out of the middle.

Someone was going to get a very stern talking to, once Sunli determined the guilty party.

In the meantime, there wasn't anything he could do. The LandHolders were arriving.

It was the first day of formal meetings between them. They had traversed Jinyi, making a grand Promenade of the city before arriving at the palace. Sunli had seen to all the details of their walk personally, making sure that they only viewed the most prosperous of neighborhoods, the largest markets and temples, before coming to the palace, ensuring that they would be suitably impressed.

The looks on their faces, though…damn it! Those flowers were just wrong. He could tell based on the glances the LandHolders kept giving the pots.

Darikuto from the House of Pearl was first. His dark skin glistened in the sunlight like he'd oiled it. He walked with pride, as if he were in line for inheriting the House of Cobalt. Sunli didn't trust the possessiveness of his gaze. He wore the traditional white, black, and silver robes of his house. It had a stiff collar that was studded with magnificent pearls down the front and sleeves.

Behind him walked Ibitsima, from the House of Crystal. She was as tall as Darikuto, her black hair braided tightly against her scalp, the skin of her face pale though her lips and cheeks had been rouged. Her gown was more practical, with slim sleeves and a well-defined waist, the tear-drop ends of it falling at mid-calf. It was done in shimmering pastels with leaves and vines embroidered in silver thread.

Unnir, from the House of Gold, came last, as was proper as she was the youngest of all the LandHolders. She walked like a gray cloud, the long open cuffs of her robe trailing behind her. Brilliant green and gold embroidered plackets lined the front. Her hair was also braided, but then the long braids had been pinned up around her head, like a crown. She looked the most severe of all of them, the most disapproving as well.

Sunli sighed again. There wasn't anything he could do about the flowerpots at that point. He'd just have to make sure they were right before their guests left.

Kinaki stood at the door of his palace in his own new

outfit. It was cobalt blue, of course, made out of the finest silk. Huge flowers were outlined in white across the fabric.

Sunli swelled with pride at how well his LandHolder looked that day. Yes, his face was redder than it had been before his illness. And the robe was voluminous. Maybe that was so Kinaki wouldn't shame the other LandHolders by displaying his mighty muscles, muscles that seemed to be growing every day.

In fact, Kinaki himself appeared to be taller as well. Normally Sunli only saw the LandHolder seated on his throne. Had he always been taller than Darikuto? Sunli wasn't certain.

No matter. The other LandHolders were sure to be impressed with what they'd seen of Jinyi, and would all privately have to agree that the House of Cobalt was the finest of all the houses.

Sunli hurried away before the LandHolders finished greeting one another. There were still so many details to be seen to! He'd had to rely on his staff more than he'd felt comfortable with, particularly now that he'd seen the fiasco of the wrong flowers out front.

But he was only one man. He couldn't be everywhere at once, no matter how often he'd bemoaned the fact.

It was up to him, though, to see that the luncheon served to the LandHolders was perfect in every detail.

No one else could manage every nuance correctly. He was certain of it.

SUNLI SAT IN HIS OFFICE, behind his desk, completely flummoxed. He didn't even know where to begin.

At least his office was clean. No dust motes danced in the sunlight coming through the far window, opposite his chair.

The small altar to the God Xiuma in the corner burned sweet incense and had a lovely collection of brilliant blue gems at his feet.

Sunli had never felt the need to be surrounded by all those books his predecessor had collected, so the shelves along the walls mostly contained beautiful geodes, rough sapphires, and other precious stones, including an arresting emerald that was still *in situ*, the top of it polished to a brilliant green surrounded by gray rock.

The desk itself had been cleaned off, all of Sunli's correspondence neatly filed in the wooden cabinet behind him. The cushions for his chair were new, cornflower blue, with a pattern of white leaves stitched across them. They weren't as comfortable as his old cushions, but he had to keep up appearances. He'd break these in over time.

The guest chair sitting across from him was empty. It was beautifully carved from a dark wood, with black leather slung for the seat and back. Honestly, it was more comfortable than Sunli's new cushions, but Sunli would not move from where he sat.

Particularly not given his most recent guest, who'd just vacated the chair in front of him.

Really, how dare that stuffy Haptomi question him? Of course, nothing was perfect, no matter how hard Sunli tried. Mistakes had been made over the course of the LandHolders' visit.

But surely that wasn't an indication that something deep at the heart of the House of Cobalt was wrong.

Was it?

Unease filled Sunli as he considered what Haptomi had said. The flowers—those were for Kinaki. He was the one who insisted on flowers now in every room of the palace. Some of them might stink, but most of them were fragrant. They weren't there to cover up a worse smell.

Were they?

And how had all those flower designs appeared in the tapestries in every room? Sunli had just assumed that the HouseHolder had overseen their addition. When he'd asked, though, the poor woman had no idea what he'd been talking about.

Just as she hadn't known about the new cushions for his chair.

No matter. One of her staff must have been more diligent than she'd expected. And after the LandHolders had left, Sunli would take the time to find out who this industrious individual was.

The flowers shouldn't make anyone anxious. They were just for show. They were merely a symbol of Kinaki's great health. Really, he had no idea what Haptomi was talking about! The flowers weren't watching people. They weren't any more aware or alive than the rest of the land.

Haptomi was just being paranoid.

Then there were the ghosts. Of course, Sunli had noticed that there weren't as many as there once had been. (Though he hadn't, not really.) But who could control the ghosts? None of the LandHolders had that ability, as Sunli had pointed out to Haptomi.

However, fewer ghosts meant less foretelling. Even Sunli had to admit that. He'd been blaming Belam for the Temple of Truth's inability to generate auguries. Belam had overstepped his bounds, asked about something that he shouldn't have. He'd "used up" all the good will of the messengers from the gods. Or at least that was the excuse that Sunli had been using since Belam's death, more than two years before.

Maybe it was something else, though. Sunli still remembered the fear etched on Belam's dead face, the rictus that only melted when the body was burned, the foul black smoke that had risen from his pyre.

What had his predecessor been up to?

Haptomi was just a stuffy old man, whining about how the House of Cobalt had changed. There wasn't really anything wrong with it or the land. It was an insult that the House of Crystal was considering leaving early. How dare Haptomi believe that his LandHolder was at risk?

But just to be on the safe side, Sunli vowed to spend the rest of the day skulking around the palace, poking his nose into all the unseen places, seeing for himself if there was anything to Haptomi's complaints or not.

Really, what more could Sunli do?

Chapter Twenty-Three
HOUSE OF GOLD

❧❧❧

EMIL WAS NOT ABOUT to admit that he was wrong. Not in public at any rate.

Particularly not if that also meant that perhaps Unnir was right. The *LandHolder*. He couldn't help but roll his eyes every time he said that, even in the privacy of his own thoughts.

Since Unnir had destroyed part of the palace while putting him and Vide in their places, Emil had walked very carefully. They'd scuttled their plans to discredit Unnir further immediately—who knew what such an emotionally unstable female LandHolder might do?

The brothers had even tried to make sure that everything went right during the House of Cobalt visit. Unnir was under enough stress as it was. Emil certainly didn't want to be flayed alive, and he had no doubt that Unnir would follow up with her threat if she mistakenly believed that either he or his brother were at fault for some of the problems that had occurred during their visit.

The first night they'd passed from their own lands into the lands controlled by the House of Cobalt, Unnir had called the brothers into her tent. She'd laid out her fears, how something was very wrong with the lands. Torja had no idea what was wrong, but had admitted that it was practically impossible to do auguries here.

Unnir had asked Emil and Vide to be her eyes and ears, to aid her in this place where she was practically blind.

Emil had strutted with pride leaving her tent. They were finally getting somewhere. The *LandHolder* was admitting how weak she was. Surely it wouldn't take that much more to convince her that she was eminently unsuited for the job and that she should just step down.

After spending a week in the House of Cobalt lands, Emil was maybe, possibly, perhaps *slightly* inclined to think that Unnir might have a point.

He wouldn't go so far as to admit that maybe the brothers needed to work together with their cousin. He had the sneaking suspicion, though, that the longer they stayed here, he might eventually come to that conclusion.

The expected knock came on his door. "Enter!" Emil called.

It was Vide, of course. They'd taken to meeting every evening just before they went to sleep, to talk about the events of the day and what they'd learned.

"Well, brother, I see that you've started without me," Vide smirked, pointing to the half-full bottle of wine sitting beside Emil.

Emil shrugged. It was a sour vintage. Or maybe that was just the bitterness of the situation, that Unnir might be right to be concerned.

"So what have you discovered?" Emil asked as Vide poured himself a glass. The room itself was nice enough, though nowhere near as fine as their rooms back in their own palace. Everything was done in reds and blacks—the rugs, the flowered tapestry hanging on the wall, even the furniture was carved out of wood stained black.

The House of Gold's colors were green, gray, and gold, with some off-white thrown in. Emil had thought that the House of Cobalt's colors were bright blue and green, the colors of cobalt, sapphire, and emerald. The amount of red and black unsettled him.

Despite the lamps hanging from the ceiling, as well as the actual burning candles that Emil had placed on the table, shadows lurked in the corners. He wasn't afraid to go into the second chamber that held his bed, afraid of the darkness there. Or so he told himself, though he did finish off a bottle of wine every evening so that he would pass out and not have more nightmares.

Vide took a sip of the wine and grimaced. Good. Maybe it wasn't just Emil's tastes being thrown off. Maybe there was something wrong with the wine. As long as it put him to sleep, he'd drink the swill.

"I talked with Kinaki's daughter today. Lijun," Vide said after a bit.

"How did you manage that?" Emil asked, surprised. It had seemed odd to the brothers that Kinaki wasn't showing off his potential heirs, that he was keeping them hidden away. He'd even sent his son off to go deal with issues of one of the major Holders.

Had there been some sort of rift in the family? Perhaps a dark secret breaking them apart?

Vide took another sip of wine and made the same grimace that he'd made the first time. "I may have hinted that the House of Gold was looking to make an allegiance with the House of Cobalt."

Emil snorted. He didn't think that Vide would actually prostitute himself that way. But his brother was considered extremely good looking and well spoken. He would certainly be considered a catch. Not that anyone as high ranking as either Emil or his brother would ever consider marrying someone from a different House. There was too good of a chance that one of their children would become LandHolder, and no one wanted to be beholden to a House other than their own.

"So what did Lijun have to say?" Emil prompted. Really, what was with his brother today? Why wasn't he smugly spilling his news as he usually did?

"She's worried about the House of Cobalt," Vide finally admitted. "She and her brother, along with their various cousins, went on Promenade earlier that year. The LandHolder never does it himself, but sends his potential heirs out."

Emil shrugged. All the houses had different habits when it came to the Promenade.

"You've heard the same things that I have about the ghosts disappearing, and that those who remain are more powerful," Vide said. "She witnessed it first-hand while traveling. But the other interesting thing she told me that we had not heard before was how Kinaki is building an army."

"We have heard that. We've heard all about that," Emil said dismissively. How Kinaki was supposedly assigning CollierHolders more warriors to fight the barbarians to the south, when everyone knew that it was just a matter of time before he directed them into the lands of the House of Gold.

"What we didn't know is how they're being trained," Vide said. He put both of his hands on the table as if he were holding himself back.

Or maybe placing his hands that way was supposed to be a distraction for Emil, who nearly missed the look of fear on his brother's face.

He'd never seen his brother look fearful before.

"New Holders have been introduced. None of the houses

have ever had WarHolders before. We have VeinHolders, the House of Pearl has PearlHolders, and there are CrystalHolders. Not dedicated WarHolders," Vide said.

Emil found his throat suddenly dry. The sourness of the wine had not gone away when he took another sip. "What else?" he said. He didn't ask what had frightened his brother. He didn't want to even admit that it was possible to scare Vide. Unnir certainly had only made his brother more cautious, not frightened.

"There are rumors, and I want to emphasize that these are only rumors from the potential heir of a rival LandHolder, that the WarHolders aren't necessarily all drawn from the living," Vide said.

"How could a ghost rule over warriors? How would they manage that?" Emil said, confused.

"Not ghosts," Vide said. He looked around the room, then leaned over the table to bring his head closer to Emil's, his voice dropping down to a whisper. "Demons."

Emil opened his mouth, then closed it again. Demons? Demons were the warriors of the Goddess Morta, set under the earth to test the souls passing through the underworld to make sure they were worthy.

A demon warrior would be a deadly foe. They would have centuries of experience fighting. They might even have their own armies of warriors, souls that they'd captured, not allowing them to leave the underworld.

"What do we do?" Emil asked as he absorbed Vide's statement. He wasn't sure if he believed it. Would demons cause so many nasty flowers to bloom all over the kingdom? Make his *LandHolder* complain that walking on the bare ground felt like walking over ashes? Destroy the ghosts and make it difficult to cast magic?

It had never been something Emil had considered before.

"We will need to tell the *LandHolder*," Vide said. He

didn't actually roll his eyes when he said it, though he held his lips pursed together afterward as if he'd just eaten the sourest of cherries.

Emil blinked, surprised. Was Vide seriously proposing that they work *with* Unnir? Instead of against her, biding their time until she could be convinced to step down, or else banished?

The seriousness of his brother's gaze left no doubt.

The brothers were going to have to swallow their pride and actually put all their considerable resources to aiding Unnir and the House of Gold.

There were evidently things afoot that were bigger than the pair of them.

Afterward, however, there was no doubt in Emil's mind that he and Vide would reverse their position and start pecking away at Unnir again.

They would help her survive this crisis. That was all.

After that, all bets were off.

Chapter Twenty-Four

HOUSE OF PEARL

CHUYOKO SAT on the floor in her rooms, looking out the window, facing west. She wore medium armor that night—heavy enough to protect her if the fighting grew fierce, but light enough so that she could run if she needed to. Her weapons lay on either side of her, a short sword on her right and a shield on her left.

She had not relaxed her training while here in Jinyi, though instead of practicing with her weapons, she spent hours working on the internal art of fighting, breathing, meditating, and extending her senses. She fought opponents in her mind, imagining every blow and deflection, perfecting her footwork and her forms.

Chuyoko was not a Holder of land. She was a PearlHolder, a warrior who protected the land. She saw herself as the armored hand that held the pearl in its palm, similar to the shell that had originally secreted it.

Tonight, it began.

Chuyoko had initially planned on being the one to strike the first blow. After two days in the lands of the House of

Cobalt, she realized that while she could insist on that honor, she had different duties to fulfill.

Fortunately, Chuyoko already had a replacement. The woman was not her second in command—what needed doing was not dependent on rank. What Chuyoko needed was fanatical obedience not just to her but to Darikuto as well.

Muramara fit the bill nicely. She was the daughter of a tavern keeper, growing up rough and always ready to brawl. Her size helped—her opponents had frequently made the mistake of thinking that someone so massive would be slow.

Chuyoko had rescued Muramara from one of the few holding pens kept by the LandHolder. She'd been brought before the Temple of Truth for destructive fighting. Muramara had actually been planning on burning down her family's tavern when her father had declared her brother as his sole heir, cutting off his daughter.

An augury had caught the crime before it had occurred, as the fire would have burned out of control and taken several buildings before those with magical power could have contained it.

Muramra's choices would normally have been banishment with her landsense stripped from her, or given hard labor. However, Chuyoko had given Muramara a third option: the opportunity to become a warrior, one of the elite handpicked squad that answered to Chuyoko alone.

The woman was now bound completely to Chuyoko, and by extension, to the LandHolder. It helped that Muramara always considered the time she'd spent since being in the pens as a gift—she should have died at that time. She'd dedicated the rest of her life to those who had allowed her to live.

Chuyoko closed her eyes as the quiet of the dark night settled in around the palace. She pushed out her senses, sliding her awareness in between the bricks of the building, through the wooden floors and around the corner towers, trying to hold the entire enclosure in her mind.

It was quite a stretch for her. That was what it felt like, too—as if she were reaching for a sword that was half an inch outside of her grasp. The building eventually allowed her presence around the edges, but she felt as though she stood with her knees bent, her arms out circling a large tree. Eventually she would tire and have to draw back.

She didn't know how the LandHolder managed to not only hold all of the lands in his head but also deal with the other Holders as well as come up with something as audacious as The Plan. Her admiration for him had tripled since coming here.

Chuyoko took another deep breath and held her metaphorical arms in place, encircling the palace. She couldn't feel all the people there, or even the land itself, just the solid structure, the weight of the bricks pressing down on one another into the earth, the sour scent of the winds that tickled its exterior, the coolness of the moonlight.

Soon, Muramara would strike. She and specially chosen comrades would first attack the guards in the palace, stealing their armor and weapons. They would each take out a guard in a different location, just after the watch had changed, so that it would be difficult later for anyone to put the pieces together.

Muramara and the others would briefly regroup outside the chambers of one of the visiting LandHolders. Then they would strike, killing everyone in that entire delegation—guards, priests, children, and eventually, the LandHolder.

It was a suicide mission. Muramara and the others knew that. The fighting would be desperate. No amount of training could prepare a warrior for the magic that would be directed at them. Even if the LandHolder wasn't in her own lands, she was still an incredible foe.

The one thing that Muramara had going for her was the corruption of the House of Cobalt. The lands here wouldn't rise to the aid of the embattled LandHolder. They might even conspire against her.

It was the degradation of the land that had worried Chuyoko enough that she had put Muramara in her place. Darikuto did not understand the full extent of the troubles here. He had believed—possibly foolishly—that he'd be able to easily cleanse this place of the demons who now lived here.

Chuyoko hadn't bothered trying to argue with him. He had enough to worry about as it was.

It was her place as the PearlHolder to take care of him. Protect him. Hold him in her hand and shelter him from all danger.

She didn't hear the first cry of pain as the first of the palace guards died. She felt it though, as if the heartbeat of the building skipped a tiny beat. It was not loud enough for anyone else to notice, possibly not even Kinaki. It was as quiet as a gasp in a room facing the ocean, the sound of the waves too loud for most to be able to hear it.

But Chuyoko had known that it was coming. She'd been waiting for that single erratic beat.

She rose from her seat, picking up her weapons. Shimokoro had not anticipated what would come next. Chuyoko didn't need to be granted a fancy augury to know, though.

There would be fighting. And fleeing.

And she was ready to defend Darikuto with her last breath.

Chapter Twenty-Five
HOUSE OF CRYSTAL

IBITSIMA SLEPT RESTLESSLY. Not just that night, but every night since passing into the lands of the House of Cobalt. She didn't understand what was wrong here, just that something was terribly, terribly wrong.

Only Unnir shared her concern. Darikuto had dismissed Ibitsima's worries, implying that her unease was due to her lack of experience as a LandHolder. It had both surprised and angered her. She hadn't been a LandHolder for a decade yet, that was true. But she had been in the position long enough to know when a land was being corrupted, even if she couldn't say exactly what had happened.

Haptomi had believed her. Despite how stuffy and formal the priest had become as he'd aged, he couldn't hide the fact that his eyes were always wide with fear. He started at the slightest noise and complained of shadows following him.

Ibitsima felt the same way. She would swear that the vines stitched into the tapestries that covered the walls moved sometimes, unfurling new leaves or blossoms. At least she'd been able to remove the pots of flowers from her rooms. The stench had given her a tremendous headache. She didn't care if they were there to "honor" the LandHolder. They were awful.

That night, Ibitsima slept alone. She'd sent her husband to his own chambers. If she could have, she would have ordered him as well as all the children back home. Immediately.

She couldn't, however. That would be too much of an insult to Kinaki, who honestly hadn't done anything wrong. Sure, there was the mix-up at dinner when his cooks had sent out food that was so amazingly spicy that no one else at the table could eat it. (Kinaki had actually taken one of the peppers and eaten it like an apple. Ibitsima had shuddered at how black his tongue had grown.)

But his cooks had tried to correct their mistake and send out more edible food, all the while Kinaki had laughed at them for being too weak. Even Darikuto hadn't been able to explain that away, or partake of the meal.

There wasn't a single instance where Kinaki had given such an insult that Ibitsima could just pack up and go. He always apologized and tried to make amends, despite his snide comments in the meantime.

Still, Ibitsima had quietly spread the word among her people to be packed up and ready to go. If they could leave even a few days early, they would.

Her bed was wide and soft, as befitted a LandHolder, with the best down mattress and well-woven sheets and blankets. It was tucked into a corner of the large bedroom. Though originally only the headboard had touched the wall beside the window, Ibitsima had pushed it into a corner. She'd laughed at herself, but she still felt better not being so exposed while she slept.

She wasn't certain what had awoken her that night. It was

as if something had bumped against her headboard, the bricks of the wall thumping with an unseen force.

Out of habit, Ibitsima reached out her senses, trying to determine what was wrong, only to be rebuffed, of course.

This damned land hated her. Hated everyone, in fact. She would bet that it hated Kinaki as well, though she doubted he realized it. He'd grown fat over the past year, like a red-faced slug that feasted on the blood of others.

She didn't trust him, or the smell of decay that lay under the cloying scent of the flowers. Her senses felt ashes and smoke everywhere, crowding in on her, as if they wanted to bury her alive.

Being here reminded her of that one winter a few years ago, when she'd woken every morning with her fingers and toes cold and numb. The main cook had fallen ill shortly after that, and with the change of cooks as well as the change of the seasons, the feeling had dissipated.

This was so much worse. She could still feel her lands, but they were distant and shadowy, as if viewed through a dark shroud.

Ibitsima listened to the quiet night for a few moments, but she didn't hear anything. Couldn't feel a sense of impending doom, or rather, no more than she'd been feeling already.

With a sigh, she turned over in her bed, snuggling under the heavy blankets, feeling chilled though she wasn't cold.

They needed to leave this place. Soon. She would pass along her regrets to Kinaki and she and her retinue would depart the day after tomorrow. It was only two days ahead of time, but every day counted in this damned land.

The decision made, Ibitsima found herself suddenly relaxing. She hadn't realized just how badly she needed to make the choice to leave here quickly, consequences be damned.

It was only as she was starting to fall back asleep that she heard the first cry for help.

WHERE WERE ALL these warriors coming from? Ibitsima felt as though they were powered by the waves of the ocean as they kept constantly pouring through her door. She destroyed them just as they crossed the threshold into her sleeping chamber, tearing their heads off or slamming their bodies to the ground, shattering their bones.

At least the smell of gore was an honest one, the taste of spilled blood almost refreshing.

Ibitsima was certain that everyone in her own guard had already been destroyed by these monsters. Her children—all the potential heirs of her land—had also been slain. Poor Haptomi hadn't really stood a chance either.

It was just her now, and she couldn't escape. The windows had sealed themselves against her, holding her in. Just a little of the night's clear air might have saved her, refreshed her enough that she could keep up her defenses until the dawn.

Something told her that she just needed to survive until sunrise. Then possibly she could be saved.

When the attack had started, she pushed against the solid wall beside her bed, seeking a way out of this trapped room.

She'd been aghast at how the wall had *flexed*, curving outward with her mighty force, then bouncing back, undamaged.

Brick was *not* supposed to be able to do that. It was supposed to be solid. These walls had acted as if they were infected with something springy, no longer made of brick but woven out of vines.

Why was Kinaki betraying her this way? Did he not

understand the repercussions of his actions? The other LandHolders would rise up against him. He wouldn't be able to withstand the combined attack of Unnir and Darikuto.

Unless Darikuto wouldn't attack. Maybe he was in collusion with Kinaki? Possibly that was why he'd dismissed her fears.

Ibitsima killed three more guards who rushed the room. She was tiring, she knew. Sooner or later they'd get through the door.

Would they kill her? Or did Kinaki have some other evil plan in store?

The next wave of guards paused outside her threshold, giving her a breather.

No, wait.

They saw what she only now noticed.

The huge tapestry that hung on the wall beside the door was growing. Or rather, the damned vines along the edges of the piece had slid past the borders of the embroidered fabric and were slowly crawling along the walls. They had breached the doorway, giving her attackers pause.

More vines and eerie plants were pushing out of the rug, with misshapen leaves and unnatural blood-red blossoms. The same horrible spiked grasses that Ibitsima had seen on her journey here pushed up suddenly, the tips seeking to impale her. She gagged as the overwhelming scent of the putrid corpse flowers started growing around the edges of the room.

Without thought, Ibitsima strengthened the shield around her. It would deflect most attacks, though eventually, it, too, would fail as her strength ran out.

When Ibitsima turned away from the door, she saw that the windows were completely screened over now with a thick mat of branches and leaves. The tapestry hanging over her bed had collapsed and now smothered where she'd been lying. Tendrils slid off the bed, their ends raised and wavering, like snakes seeking their prey.

Ibitsima made one last attempt to free herself. She raised her hands and set fire to the vegetation choking the window. It was the clearest area. She needed to be able to breathe the free air, just for a moment.

The smoke bellowed, nasty and oily, quickly filling the room. Ibitsima kept a bubble of air around herself as she pushed forward. She dug at the plants with powerful magic, trying to tear them apart. They felt thick and slimy even though she didn't touch them physically.

Sweat gathered along her back and ran down her spine. She tried blasting the vines with cold, drawing on the chill of the snow-peaked mountains of her home. The plants turned to ash which whirled around, drawing power to itself.

Given enough time, Ibitsima knew that it would coalesce into yet another being that would attack.

Ibitsima returned her attention to the window. She could see the clear night outside. She just had to punch through the thick glass, shatter it so that the wind might carry her cries to someone, anyone, who could help.

A pain in her side made her look down.

Though the warriors had stayed on their side of the threshold, that hadn't stopped them from throwing spears at her.

Of course, most had been blocked by her own personal shield.

But a thread of ivy from the floor had wormed its way under her protective barrier, weakened it. A single spear had gotten through.

Ibitsima blasted those on the other side of the door without turning to look. She couldn't afford to lose her focus on the window.

The glass vibrated with the pounding magic she poured

out. Even magically enhanced, the covering on the window could only hold out for so long.

The loud sound of glass shattering filled the room. Ibitsima took a deep breath of the cool air streaming in.

It was too late, though, for that fresh air to revive her. Even if she did manage to hold on until morning, she wouldn't survive.

She focused all her attention outward. She didn't bother trying to touch the land or draw its power into herself—the earth here was too foreign, too corrupted.

Instead, Ibitsima focused on the other LandHolders, on Unnir and Darikuto. She tried to warn them of her fate, to let them know that they were about to undergo the same.

The only way to save themselves was to flee. Now. The pair of them would have to reunite later in order to destroy Kinaki and the terrible demons who had taken over his land.

Or was it even Kinaki anymore? Had he become a demon himself? She wondered now, with his red face and constantly shifting torso.

Her warning winging away, Ibitsima turned to face her foes. Instead of warriors, she now faced monsters, as she'd suspected all along would be her fate.

She fought bravely and well, knowing with the accuracy of augury that she was as doomed as had been all her people.

It struck her as funny, that at the end of her life her last thoughts weren't of the land but of its people.

Maybe her father had been right. Maybe people were more important than the land.

She still didn't fully understand the sentiment. Perhaps given enough years and more wisdom, she could have. But she was out of time.

When the demon's sword finally pierced her shield and cleaved her head from her body, Ibitsima felt the mantle of the Land lift off her shoulders. She imagined it flying away, quickly crossing the lands of the House of Gold, settling on the shoulders of the one she'd left behind.

Akalina.

Then Ibitsima knew no more of what occurred above the ground.

Chapter Twenty-Six
HOUSE OF COBALT

AFTER THE DISASTROUS meeting with Haptomi, Sunli spent the afternoon wandering around the palace, trying to see what his counterpart was seeing.

So maybe the amount of flowers scattered in the various rooms was a lot. They just showed the wealth of the LandHolder! Sunli did have to admit that the tapestries were slightly creepy, and he did wonder why the vines that had been stitched along the edges appeared to move now and again.

But that was just a sign of the LandHolder's great magic. Wasn't it?

The kitchen left Sunli uneasy. When had the cooks stopped making plain bread? He vaguely recalled some complaints about it, but he hadn't really been paying attention. His own personal chef had made sure that Sunli was fed properly. Yet, all the bread pans were empty and the oven reserved for making bread for the household was cold.

Had the cooks always had such red faces before? They looked a little like the LandHolder in that aspect. He tried to tell himself that it was just the heat of the ovens, but their appearance didn't sit well with him. There was something off about them.

Unfamiliar haunches of meat hung from the rafters, making the kitchen seem like a foreign hunter's cabin. Strong herbs and hot peppers filled the pots beside the kitchen window, growing as profusely as the flowers in the rest of the palace. Large woven baskets sat beside every table, rustling with whatever they contained.

Sunli still regretted lifting the top of one and seeing the fat white slugs writhing there. He wasn't sure when he'd have an appetite again.

Perhaps the slugs would be considered a delicacy for some. They'd just turned Sunli's stomach. Plus, they were still coated in dirt and slime. He just knew that the cooks wouldn't bother washing the insects at all. They might even be served live.

Sunli hadn't bothered lifting the lids on any of the rest of the baskets, having seen enough.

Something was definitely wrong if that was what the LandHolder now ate.

There were probably other things wrong with the palace, things that Sunli hadn't bothered to see. There wasn't anyone he could ask. Not even Benitoyo, as the merchant had always laughed away any of Sunli's previous fears.

No, Sunli knew what he needed to do, as much as he might dread it.

He needed to try to cast an augury, to find out just exactly how bad things had gotten.

THE TEMPLE OF TRUTH was in the palace compound, though close to the wall. Sunli hurried there as the sun was just starting to set. Behind the temple, a set of stairs ran underground to the augury room.

Sunli had ordered the original augury room to be filled with stone and sealed, and a second room to be carved out. However, he personally hadn't returned underground since Belam had died. Instead, he'd done what few auguries he'd attempted in rooms above ground.

Sunli took it as a good sign that he could easily light one of the prepared rocks next to the stairs going down, was able to easily perform the necessary magic to keep the dark away. However, as he walked down the stairs his confidence vanished. The lighted rock, though it hadn't faded, was actually barely keeping away the darkness down here. It was as if shadows crowded around him.

He shivered as he stepped off the stone stairs and onto the dirt floor. The space around the end of the stairs opened up, like a small vestibule, wide enough for four men. Had this place always been so chilly? He didn't recall that. Really, it was as if all the ghosts from the palace had gathered down here to hide.

The lighted rock in his hand appeared to flicker, as though it were a flaming torch in a high wind. Sunli lifted it high above his head to see better. The darkness shrank back, slowly retreating, like a black tide.

The wall directly to Sunli's left had a dark door-shape. That was the entrance to the former augury room. Just beyond that stood an actual wooden door, reinforced with black iron. The door handle was made of brass, the plate behind it studded with beautiful polished rocks.

It surprised Sunli that the door was locked. He didn't recall ordering such a thing. He tried turning the cold handle again, even tugging on the door hard enough to rattle it in its frame, but it wouldn't budge.

Strange.

He couldn't help the relief he felt. Maybe this was the gods' way of telling him that he shouldn't try casting an augury down here.

Sunli turned to go back up the stairs when a quiet warm wind whispered around him, stopping him in his tracks.

No wind should ever be found this far under the earth.

He stood frozen with fear as the stone covering the entrance to the first augury room, the one where Belam died, melted away like thick fog. Reddened lights shone out into the hallway. The smell of sulfur and dried bones wafted out.

Despite his growing terror, Sunli found himself walking forward, first up to the entrance, then through it, into the old augury room.

The cold in the hallway gave way immediately to heat. Ghostly flames raged in wavery braziers set at the end of the room. The smell of foul smoke increased, though Sunli knew that he was only seeing shadows—no augury fires actually burned here.

A figure stepped out from behind the black pots. It took Sunli a few moments to recognize that it was Belam, his former mentor.

"Ah, Sunli," Belam said, his voice as indistinct as any ghost's. "Why have you come?"

"I needed to see the truth for myself," Sunli said. "I needed to learn what was actually happening in the palace. In the lands. With the LandHolder."

He hadn't meant to say so much, but there appeared to be some sort of *geas* on him in this place, where he was compelled to speak the full truth.

"You want to see?" Belam asked, sliding across the room. He didn't walk like a person, but floated like a ghost.

As he drew closer, Sunli could see that Belam didn't look

like a ghost. The smoke that had coalesced into his body had turned black. His eyes shone like a sickly moon, yellow with pus. Though his mouth moved as he talked, his face seemed taut, as if still caught in the rictus of fear that had killed him.

"Yes," Sunli said, still obliged to tell the truth. "I want to see."

He regretted the words as soon as he said them. Particularly given the predatory grin that Belam gave him.

"Then you shall see," Belam said. His form dissolved into pure smoke that wrapped itself around Sunli, trapping him in its burning embrace.

Sunli tried to call out but found he couldn't make a sound. Plus, opening his mouth allowed the smoke inside of him. Sunli struggled to free himself. He pushed out with his arms only to find them tightly bound around his torso. He tried to run, but immediately tripped and fell hard on his knees. He blinked, his eyes watering, his mouth tasting of ashes. His ears rang as though his screams hadn't been silenced.

Belam slipped inside of Sunli, as intimate as a lover, wrapping around Sunli's silvery soul. It surprised Sunli how strongly his soul still shone, despite being wrapped so tightly in ash and stone. He maintained a sliver of himself even with the soul of a demon now trapped inside of him.

Ah, came the whispered words of Belam. *You are stronger than I'd thought.*

Sunli took encouragement from that. He was strong. He could be stronger than anyone had expected.

But now you shall see, Belam promised.

Sunli found he suddenly had control of his limbs. He raced out of the room and up the stairs.

Guards called to one another as he emerged. Was the palace under attack?

The heaving walls of the buildings around Sunli made him shudder. No brick remained, just a writhing mass of sickly vegetation with a mind of its own. Great pits sundered the earth. Not ghosts, but demons, roamed widely.

He no longer lived in a palace, but in the underworld raised above the ground.

Chapter Twenty-Seven
HOUSE OF GOLD

TORJA IGNORED how her stomach rumbled. It had been three days since solid food had passed her lips. She'd abstained from all the feasts being thrown in Jinyi, sticking close to her rooms in Kinaki's palace. She subsisted on broth and watered wine. She took cold baths twice a day, plunging headlong into the chilled water. She prayed almost the entire time, the words of her pleas echoing and chasing her even during her short sleeps.

Finally, she was ready to try the next augury. Ragna had tended her the entire time of her purification, and now led her from her assigned room in the palace of the House of Cobalt to the gazebo out back.

Winds blew roughly against Torja's skin. The night felt thick and heavy. Torja ignored the scent of the damned flowers growing back here. Even with her empty stomach they still made her queasy.

Torja had gone through every ancient text on auguries and divination that she could find, first at the House of Gold, now, in the House of Cobalt. In times of great need, other priests and priestesses had tried fasting as she had, along with mixing forms of augury.

Tonight was Torja's most desperate attempt to find out what exactly was going on, not just in the House of Gold, but here also.

Though Torja knew it was her overly active imagination, she couldn't help but remember the Bandit SlugHolder who had stolen her one *fletche*, and how Kinaki resembled that slug, with his fat face and grotesque body. They were intimately connected in her fevered brain, and she kept circling back to them.

She should have burned those *fletche* when she started having problems with auguries. She'd tried other sets. But those had been her favorite.

Tonight it was time to try once again to use that original set and see if she could finally discover the root cause of their problems.

The gazebo had been prepared according to the ancient ritual. A hole had been cut in the center of the roof for the smoke to billow directly up. The walls were all painted brilliant white, unmarred and pure. Torja herself was in a white sheath dress, sleeveless and unadorned. She'd bound her hair up on top of her head, held there with sharp thorns that pricked her scalp.

Torja held Ragna's arm until the first step leading up to the prepared space. Then she stopped and turned to her assistant. "Thank you," she said, her voice hoarse from days of praying.

"You must succeed," Ragna said, her own voice a whisper. "I don't trust what is going on here. I don't trust my senses. We need to know what happened."

Torja nodded. Ragna had turned into a good accomplice for their distressing times, willing to put aside their differences for the good of the land and its Holder.

It helped that Torja was willing to undergo all manner of purging and purification in order to give them the divination they so desperately needed. Ragna wouldn't have gone so far, and had admitted it more than once. She knew that Torja was the right leader of the Temple of Truth.

At least for now.

Torja slowly walked up the three stairs to the floor of the gazebo, holding herself rigidly straight. She thankfully sank back down to the hard floor in front of the brazier, however. She was so weak.

The squat brazier was two feet tall and about the same wide. Sacred wood and incense were nestled at the bottom of it. The brazier itself was made out of black iron and stood on four solid feet. A design of braided wheat went around the top lip. The handles also appeared to be made out of the same pattern.

Torja faced the east. The ancient texts had never agreed on which cardinal direction was the most important. All that mattered was that that was the direction she felt most comfortable in.

Using an already lit candle, Torja set the wood and incense before her on fire. The wood caught quickly, its smoke sweet. Blue-green flames quickly covered it. It took longer for the incense to catch. It was made from a resin of a tree, and to Torja's fevered eyes, looked like dirty brown crystals.

Torja continued her unending prayers to the gods, naming them one after another, begging for their help in parting the veils, to seeing the truth of what had happened. The smoke made her dizzy. Even with the cool night air, she was soon sweating as she pleaded.

Finally, Torja reached to the side for her *fletche*, her original set. It pained her to throw them into the fire, but she was more than willing to make the sacrifice. One by one the braided pieces of wheat went into the brazier, each sparking with strange blue flames as they were consumed.

Though Torja had no way of knowing for certain which of the *fletche* had been the one carried away by the slug, she still felt that one of the *fletche* carried something within it, and reserved that one for last.

After waving the last *fletche* over the brazier, she tossed it in. The small braid of wheat caught fire as the others had, soon reduced to ash.

Torja stared at the smoke rising from the brazier. She didn't see anything there. No visions coalesced out of the flames.

Damn it! This had to work.

She found herself swaying, continuing to pray even as the flames were starting to die out.

Without meaning to, Torja slumped forward, bringing her face closer to the brazier. She took in a large lungful of smoke. Her eyes started watering. The skin on her face burned from the heat.

A sliver of a vision appeared before her. Kinaki without his magnificent blue robes, his body grown fat and segmented. Something appeared to be wrapped around his torso. But what?

Torja coughed, and leaned back. The vision disappeared.

No! That couldn't happen. She had to see.

She pushed herself forward again, setting her face right above the brazier, letting the smoke overtake her. Her skin burned and she couldn't breathe.

But she must see!

Torja willed herself to stay where she was, breathing in the smoke as the visions continued.

A great snakelike being inhabited Kinaki's body with him. Its body wrapped around his, its head sitting beside his own, whispering in his ear.

Though Torja had never seen such a thing, her vision told her the truth.

The LandHolder was possessed by a demon from the underworld.

That wasn't all.

Torja felt her soul leave her body and begin to walk around the palace.

It, too, was possessed. The walls were no longer solid. Great pits of burning fire ran along cracks in the fine roads in the palace complex. Ghosts had been herded into a pen, somehow imprisoned there by demon guards, their souls feeding the demons until one by one, they were being completely consumed.

The flowers were the key, and part of the demonic possession. They all needed to be burned or magically destroyed. Just plowing them under the earth would only allow them to spread.

Torja heard someone calling her name. The voice sounded far away. One part of her recognized that it was Ragna, concerned that Torja was no longer breathing.

But Torja couldn't come back. Not yet. There was something else the vision had for her. One other scene for her to see.

Darikuto? He had known. He had a great book in front of him that had warned of this.

And he had done nothing.

Worse, he'd used the knowledge in this book to corrupt Kinaki.

Fine metal pins, like fishhooks, sank into Torja's shoulders, trying to draw her back from the brink. She had to breathe. Her lungs demanded it. Painful blisters had already formed on her face.

Though Torja tried to hold onto the visions, her body could no longer sustain the contact. She knew it was Ragna who pulled her back, Ragna who laid her abused body on the floor of the gazebo.

One last vision came as Torja coughed and the pain sank into her bones.

Ibitsima fighting off demons in her chamber.

And losing.

"We're under attack," Torja managed to wheeze out. "You must warn the LandHolder. Flee."

"Not without you," Ragna said, determined to make Torja sit, pulling at her deadened body.

She nearly protested. Saving Unnir was more important.

But Torja had hard-earned visions to share. Information the LandHolder needed.

Her mother had always said that she had an extra share of stubborn.

Torja didn't know how she made herself stand, weak and dizzy as she was, but she did. Aftereffects of her vision flickered across her sight, making her shy away from the walls and around the pits waiting to capture them.

She would make it to the LandHolder. She would tell her what she'd seen.

Most importantly, she would warn Unnir about Darikuto. He wasn't to be trusted.

If they made it out of the House of Cobalt lands alive.

Chapter Twenty-Eight
HOUSE OF PEARL

✦

DARIKUTO HAD to admit that perhaps there was a flaw with The Plan.

Kinaki had been corrupted. What Darikuto hadn't counted on was how far the corruption would go, how the land, itself, reflected the LandHolder's possession.

In retrospect, Darikuto should have foreseen this, that of course, the land reflected the state of the LandHolder. Except that when he fell ill, the land didn't ail. No, it merely found itself a new Holder. He had contingency plans for that.

He had not planned for this much success.

The other LandHolders were uneasy. Darikuto had tried to make light of their concerns, while secretly sharing them himself.

Now, tonight, they would be able to put everything to right. One of Chuyoko's warriors, dressed like Kinaki's guards, would kill Ibitsima. The other LandHolders would be appalled. The three of them would be able to force Kinaki aside. Kill not only him, but all his heirs, so that Darikuto could assume the power of his lands.

Then he would race the very winds themselves to claim the lands of the House of Crystal.

Unnir, alone and isolated, would give in to Darikuto's demands that she surrender her lands to him as well over the following year.

Darikuto sat alone in his sleep chamber meditating. He wore light sleeping robes despite the chill of the night. Like the others, he'd had the flowers removed. He'd also taken down the tapestries that night, rolled them up and stashed them outside his rooms, as well as the rugs. He appreciated the bare brick and the strong walls surrounding him, as well as the solid wood floor. The window had a dark glaze that hid the night outside.

Though Kinaki had thought it strange, Darikuto had also had the desk removed from his room. The only thing that remained was a bed, pushed up against the corner. This left adequate room for Darikuto to do his warrior practice in the center of the space, as well as a clear spot for him to sit and meditate.

Darikuto stretched his senses out. He didn't know if he'd be able to feel when Ibitsima died. All the potential heirs being slain would make her land restless.

If everything went according to The Plan, the only potential heir would be back at the House of Crystal. He or she would be young and untrained. The land might not even settle on them, but hold itself back for ten to fourteen days. If Darikuto arrived during that time, he knew the spells that would enable him to wrestle the land away from another, to bind it to himself.

Was the night restless? Or was it just Darikuto? He found his thoughts darting this way and that, like small gnats gliding over a pond, wanting to dive in but afraid of drowning.

He thought he might have felt the moment that Ibitsima

died. There appeared to be a pause in the quiet, a soft gasp.

Good. Now he could rest and wait until morning, when he and the other LandHolders would confront Kinaki.

Darikuto rose and stretched. The next step of The Plan was complete. He needed to sleep now and be ready for the upcoming battle.

Before he could make it back to his bed, Chuyoko burst through Darikuto's door. She was dressed in armor, carrying a bloodied blade.

"We need to go," she said. She didn't bow her head, but stepped boldly into his room, glancing around the chamber.

"What do you mean?" Darikuto said. "What happened?"

Chuyoko left his sleeping chamber and walked back into the sitting room, flinging open the cabinet holding Darikuto's clothes. "Ibitsima is dead," Chuyoko said. "Kinaki's guards are attacking all the LandHolders."

"What?" Darikuto said, still confused. Why would Kinaki's guards attack the other LandHolders? It had been Darikuto's warriors who had killed Ibitsima, right?

Chuyoko thrust Darikuto's heaviest robe toward him. "Put this on."

A soft cry rent the air. Darikuto started. Chuyoko threw the robe at him and raced toward the door.

Only now did Darikuto see that Chuyoko had her guards posted at his entrance. They talked together in low, urgent voices before Chuyoko turned back to Darikuto. "We should be able to clear a path through the southern gate," she told him. "That's still the least protected."

The expression on her face told him that she would brook no argument from him. If he refused, she would actually pick him up and throw him over her shoulder to get him free of the palace.

"All right," Darikuto said. He slid the heavy robe over the one he was already wearing. Chuyoko handed him a sword.

He knew that she didn't expect him to have to use it except in the most desperate of circumstances. She and her warriors would see that he was safe.

It was a measure of how serious the fighting was that Chuyoko would arm the LandHolder.

"What about Shimokoro and the others?" Darikuto said as he followed Chuyoko to the doorway.

"I have teams collecting them," Chuyoko said. One of her warriors raised a fist, then pointed down the hallway. "This way."

Darikuto felt Chuyoko's warriors hustling him down the hall. That there were dead bodies dressed in Kinaki's uniforms surprised him.

Why was Kinaki attacking? What had spurred him to act? The attack on Ibitsima was supposed to be an isolated incident, meant to disrupt the LandHolder, not fling him into action.

It was only when Darikuto took a closer look at the face of one of the guards that he realized his mistake.

The face was red and swollen. The eyes which were still open were huge and a sickly yellow color. A massive black tongue protruded from the guard's mouth. Instead of a nose, he had a snout, festooned with open sores. His ears folded at the top, like a pig's.

The body hadn't been a living being, but a demon who'd taken over the poor man's flesh.

Darikuto swallowed hard against a suddenly dry throat.

How many of Kinaki's guards had been possessed? How many of them now fought for the being that owned Kinaki's soul instead of for the LandHolder himself?

Darikuto gripped the sword he held more tightly.

The Plan to corrupt Kinaki had been more successful than he'd ever dreamed possible.

Far more than he'd ever planned for.

Chapter Twenty-Nine
HOUSE OF CRYSTAL

AKALINA WASN'T sure what woke her. She still wore her virginal nightgown, the white forever unmarred. Ibitsima and the others would be returning from the House of Cobalt in a week's time. Then, Akalina would know her full status.

At least they wouldn't banish her. Akalina was fairly certain of that. She had too good of a landsense for that. Instead, she'd be inducted into one of the temples, perhaps even the Temple of Truth, as she had such a strong connection with the ghosts.

She couldn't return to her parents. They'd made that abundantly clear, practically disowning her.

It surprised Akalina that their disappointment hadn't cut more deeply. Then again, she'd always known that they considered her more of a tool and less of a daughter to them ever since she'd attended the court of the ghosts.

She still thought about the night with the knife. She didn't regret her decision...most of the time. She'd already packed all her belongings in her room, prepared to be sent to the temple immediately upon Ibitsima's return.

Akalina lay in her bed shivering, though the night wasn't

cold. She hadn't been having a nightmare, not anything she remembered. She lit a candle with just a thought, aware that for many, that tiny bit of magic seemed to have fled.

Ghosts huddled in the corners of her room, barely visible in the dim light. It was strange how much the appearance of the ghosts had changed, grown less distinct over the past couple of years. Akalina could hear them whispering urgently to themselves.

Had the ghosts awakened her? What was wrong with them?

A dark shadow flew across Akalina's bed, as though a cloud had crossed the bright path of the sun. Akalina sat up, startled.

"What is it?" she asked the ghosts directly. "What is happening?"

A great sigh filled the chamber.

Then Akalina felt it.

Ibitsima was dead.

Everyone in the land had heard her death cry. She hadn't died peacefully. Violence had been done to her.

What had happened in the House of Cobalt? Who had attacked Ibitsima?

A second cloud approached Akalina's bed. It looked like a brown cape, winging its way across the open space of her room, floating in front of her.

It took Akalina a moment to recognize that this was a form of the Land itself, a manifestation of the power of the LandHolder.

She held her breath when the cape flew over her head then settled on her shoulders.

It felt cold. Oh, so cold. As though wet freezing blankets had just been wrapped around Akalina's soul.

This was what the LandHolder bore? How?

Akalina learned much in those few moments of being

embraced by the Land. How all of her cousins had also been slain. How no other heir in that foreign place was suitable. The power of the Land had fled back to where it belonged.

The House of Cobalt was overrun with demons. The land there was corrupted beyond measure.

Akalina tried to warm the Land surrounding her, tried to hold onto it and draw it further into her soul.

A second spike of ice, like a dagger in her belly, made her cry out.

That was when Akalina knew that Rosahaptu had deliberately made Akalina barren. The Land sensed that, could feel her lack.

With regret, the Land lifted itself off Akalina's shoulders. She felt bereft, abandoned by that which she loved most of all.

A thread of the Land remained with her, though. At least long enough for her to feel it fly far to the north and attempt to settle on another's shoulders.

Yimifut. The boy who had spoken too much truth.

The Land remained unsettled, though.

Had he rejected it? Why?

His words came streaking back to Akalina, how she would be the only one to survive.

She gasped. He'd been right.

Why had he refused the Land? Why wouldn't he become the next LandHolder?

Had he foreseen some awful future if he took the mantle of the Land?

Akalina didn't know. All she could tell was that the Land no longer had a Holder.

And it was growing wild.

Chapter Thirty
HOUSE OF COBALT

KINAKI DRANK HEAVILY THAT NIGHT, attempting to forget the looks of shocked disgust on his guests' faces from dinner.

They just didn't appreciate the efforts that his cooks had gone to. They were weak, unable to handle the spices that he loved. They didn't understand how much greater he'd become, not just Holder of the land but also of the underworld.

It didn't matter to him that the other LandHolders were so different from him, that he was on his own. Never completely alone, as Wanho was constantly there, whispering in his ear.

Sometimes Kinaki missed his solitude. Wanho would grow silent for a few hours at those times, giving Kinaki the opportunity to breathe the air freely.

He tried to ignore how it was always tainted with smoke, a smell that seemed to be growing steadily.

That night, Wanho seemed restless. Kinaki felt the great demon's anxiety prickling his own skin. There were just a few days left of the LandHolder's visit. They'd all expressed some level of concern for Kinaki and his land, trying to subtly ask questions.

Too bad. At least he'd gotten a good look at Unnir. She was isolated from her cousins, who spread nasty rumors about her every chance they got. The head priestess of her House of Truth was weak and useless, actually admitting to having problems with divination.

Unnir would be easy to take. His warriors would sweep over her lands next year while she was in the House of Pearl lands. Though honestly, would she even be able to direct her forces if she were seated on her throne? The woman had no skill or backbone. She was as good as gone.

Ibitsima was a worry. Of all the LandHolders, she was the strongest in her cold mountainous lands. Wanho had assured Kinaki that she would pose no threat to him and his armies, though.

Kinaki had wearily corrected the demon once again that they were *their* warriors. Not his alone.

He took another sip of his wine, feeling it going to his head. He'd taken to drinking heavily every night, something that Wanho appeared to relish. The LandHolder emptied his third bottle of fortified wine and reached for the fourth when something outside his rooms made a strange clicking sound, like an empty glass being lightly tapped with a metal fork.

What was that? Kinaki put down the next bottle and stood. Wanho tightened his grasp around Kinaki's torso, as if he, too, had heard the noise.

Kinaki didn't bother asking Wanho about it. The demon didn't always tell Kinaki the truth, something he'd come to accept as just part of his life.

A shout resounded in the hallway outside of Kinaki's room.

Was that one of his guards? Kinaki rushed to the door, but found he couldn't open it.

It's to keep you safe, Wanho assured him.

"Safe from what?" Kinaki demanded.

No reply.

Kinaki sent his senses through the floor of his room, seeking to discover what was going on inside his own damned palace.

The walls pushed back, hindering his movement.

What in the name of the Tombs of Granite was this nonsense?

Instead of traveling easily along the mortar of the bricks, it felt as if he traveled across mats of grass, not woven together but grown chaotically, the ends pricking him as he moved along.

What were his guards doing, fighting Ibitsima? Why were they attacking another LandHolder?

No. Wait.

Those weren't his guards. There was nothing human left inside of any of them.

They'd been taken over, as he had been. Not by Wanho but by Wanho's own warriors.

"Why?" Kinaki cried, the word echoing through his closed-off chamber.

It was time, Wanho stated simply.

"I was going to wait a year."

Kinaki felt the demon shrug in a mostly human manner.

All the LandHolders were here. Best to strike now.

Kinaki shook his head. "You won't kill them all. They'd band together and attack. We can't withstand their combined force."

The chuckle that Wanho gave sent a shiver down Kinaki's spine.

They'll never trust each other enough.

Darikuto had been planning to kill Ibitsima? And blame it on him?

Kinaki burned with anger. "Kill them. Kill them all," he directed.

With pleasure.

Kinaki felt Wanho's attention turn away from him, directed outward to the other LandHolders and the battles taking place.

It bothered Kinaki that he could barely feel what was happening in his own palace. It was as if his control of it had seeped away, the grasses overgrowing the brick, while he'd been lulled into complacency.

Without meaning to, Kinaki shivered.

Wasn't this what Kinaki had wanted all along? To be the single LandHolder? To have his will over not just all the lands, but all the underworld as well?

Something still unsettled him enough to cause him to break into a cold sweat.

He was the one in charge of their body. Only he could speak. Yet, somehow, Wanho had managed to coordinate and direct this attack.

Without Kinaki.

How much did the demon need the LandHolder?

And for how long?

Chapter Thirty-One
HOUSE OF GOLD

❧

UNNIR BIT her tongue and didn't say anything when she saw Torja's condition. Though it took much effort, she managed to bring at least some healing to the poor woman's ravaged face. Torja had burned off her eyebrows, as well as her eyelashes. Ugly blisters still oozed around her nose. But at least she was no longer a nightmare, with strips of skin hanging from what little remained of her face.

Unnir listened to the priestess' confession while she worked, how Torja, Ragna, and the others had lied about the auguries that they'd "foretold," how all those in the Temple of Truth had worked together to deceive the LandHolder while they tried more and more extreme forms of divination.

The news that Kinaki had been possessed by a demon actually made sense to Unnir. She'd known there was something wrong with his lands the moment she'd set foot in them.

More remarkable, her cousins had even come to her and agreed that she'd been right to be worried and they were pledging their full support to her.

It was likely to be the only good thing that came from this trip.

"We need to leave. Now," Torja had insisted when she'd first arrived at Unnir's rooms.

Unnir had nodded to her servants. They'd started throwing bags together, packing quickly. They wouldn't try to take everything they'd brought with them. Instead, they made packs that could be easily carried on their backs.

Emil and Vide had come in while Torja had still been talking, the LandHolder still fixing her face.

Emil's blanched appearance had almost made Unnir laugh. Poor boy wasn't used to seeing others in pain. He didn't understand that as LandHolder, she felt it constantly.

And possibly that had been one of the reasons why the land hadn't chosen him as LandHolder, his inability to feel empathy.

Her uncle had certainly been able to feel the emotions of others. He just hadn't cared. Or the only emotions that he delighted in were pain and fear.

By the time Torja had wound down and her face mostly healed, Unnir was ready to go.

"Leave behind anything that isn't light and easy to carry," she directed. "We fly. Now."

At first, Unnir had difficulty breaking the windows in her room. The glass appeared to resist her efforts. Was it no longer glass? She directed an intense cone of fire at it, eventually burning off the magic that held it solid. She heard the slight gasp of shock from her cousins and smiled grimly.

They still had no idea of the true power of a LandHolder.

The glass finally shattered. A cry of pain swept in on the night air that filled the room.

Ibitsima. Warning the other LandHolders that they must flee.

Unnir nodded and gathered those in the room to her.

She spread her magic around them, lifting the group up and flying them out the window.

If she could have pulled any power from the land, she might have been able to carry them all the way back to the House of Gold. As it was, she only managed to deposit them safely just past the gates of the palace.

The guards spread out around the group. Torja cried out, warning of the coming plague.

Large beetles descended on them, each about the length of a palm. They had sharp mandibles, able to tear out chunks from flesh. The warriors stood confused, unable to bash anything with their swords. Instead, Emil, Vide, and Unnir tried to set flame to every beetle that landed.

"We have to keep going!" Torja called as she flung beetles away from her. "There are guards coming for us!"

Unnir shuddered at the sound the black bodies made as she stepped on them. She was going to completely exhaust her power before the end of the night. Hopefully, she had enough to move them to safety.

With a great effort, Unnir moved the group down the road. It would help once they started walking on their own. Right now, it felt to her like picking up a huge sack of gold, unwieldly and heavy, then swinging it so it landed a few feet away.

"Walk!" she urged everyone. "Keep walking!"

The next step was easier as people found their cadence. She multiplied every step, as she'd done on their trip there.

Would it be enough?

Black clouds poured out of the palace gates behind them. The beetles fell away and the smell of certain death reached them.

Choking and coughing, Unnir kept the group moving forward. Two of her warriors deliberately turned away, staying behind to fight the demons.

Unnir felt their souls pass as she moved up the road.

She didn't have many more guards whom she could lose.

The land itself turned against her. Those awful spiked grasses grew sharp barbs that tore into flesh as they passed. Vines grew thick as ropes to trip them up. The choking scent of corpse flowers coalesced into gassy fog, causing them all to gag.

And still, the black cloud behind them rolled on.

Unnir didn't think she'd be able to fight it if it caught them.

Each breath took more effort as the group fled. Each step as well.

Unnir felt herself falter. She would have fallen to the ground had Emil not stepped beside her and caught her elbow.

"Thank you," she whispered, focused on taking the group forward again. Her legs grew leaden. It was difficult to raise her feet up, to take that next step.

"Here, cousin," Emil said. He took her hand, intertwining their fingers, then squeezing.

Unnir nodded, intuitively grasping what he was offering.

His strength for all of them.

She drew quickly from him, pushing them all further forward. The next step, and the one after that, were miles apart, not merely yards.

Vide took Unnir's other hand. She didn't have the breath to tease him about not wanting to be left out, how he didn't want Emil to be the only hero of the night.

She still threw him a grateful smile.

With the combined strength of the three of them, Unnir pushed the small retinue ahead further and faster, through the endless night. Howls pursued them, as well as foul winds.

But Unnir's target was close.

Just as the life giving sun crested the horizon, Unnir took

one last step, pushing the group over the border between the House of Cobalt and the House of Gold.

Unnir paused, soaking up the good, clean power of her lands. The air was no longer tainted with smoke. Her muscles ached with all the lifting she'd done, but it would only take hours now for her to heal, not weeks.

She turned toward the dark cloud still racing toward them, as if it thought it could bowl her over.

No. She was not as weak as the rest of them believed.

Unnir stomped her foot down. This was *her* land. She was the LandHolder. Everything here obeyed her.

Everything.

A golden curtain suddenly rose up along the border, towering over her head. It shimmered in the early morning light, swaying in the soft breeze.

Though the curtain looked as though a strong breeze could blow it away, it actually was a shield that would protect her and her land from any who meant her harm.

The black cloud hurled itself against the barrier. Unnir heard the sound of rocks being thrown against a wall. Harsh winds abraded the skin on her face. The smell of corruption followed.

Unnir swallowed against a dry throat. She'd turned back this attack, at least for now.

It wouldn't be the last.

"Come," she said, drawing her group together. She passed along as much strength to them as she could. They needed to get back to Haravik, the capital city, to prepare for the coming war.

Emil and Vide nodded to her, their expressions grim. They understood the battles that were to come. In that moment, they both pledged her their strength and support.

Without them, the House of Gold didn't stand a chance.

With them, there was still too great a chance that they'd lose.

But Unnir would fight with the last breath of her body to keep her lands pure and clean.

She had to. That was what the LandHolder did. Whether or not she was up to the task.

Chapter Thirty-Two

HOUSE OF PEARL

SHIMOKORO STOOD on the hillside gasping with the others. It had been a long hard fight out of Jinyi. They'd lost many warriors, their souls consumed, eaten by their enemies to fuel them.

Chuyoko had ensured their safety. He was still amazed at the tiny warrior woman who'd appeared to be all places at once, defending them like the Goddess Morta made flesh. She moved as fast as storm winds, whirling around the group, fighting on all sides, against both demons and the horrible vegetation that seemed to have a mind of its own.

Darikuto had helped, using his magic to slide the group along, making every step count as three. But the land had sapped his strength and will. Only Shimokoro and Chuyoko had ensured that Darikuto had kept moving along.

It worried Shimokoro.

Now, just after dawn, the group stood in the foothills west of the House of Cobalt, across the border. Darikuto had straightened up immediately, taking in the strength of his land. Belatedly, he'd remembered to push some of that healing power out to the others, aiding them.

Shimokoro took a deep breath. The air was still polluted with the scent of decay, rotting marshes and rancid meat. Though they were in the lands of the House of Pearl, he still felt uneasy, as if the underworld far beneath their feet teemed with warriors seeking a way to break free.

He turned to look at Darikuto. The LandHolder had a gleam in his eye that Shimokoro didn't trust. He seemed eager to return to the House of Cobalt, tempted to take a step forward and be consumed by it.

Finally, Darikuto shook his head, breaking whatever spell that foul land had cast on him.

"What now?" Chuyoko said, asking the question that was on all of their minds as usual.

"We still have The Plan," Darikuto said. "There need to be some adjustments made to it. But I will still be the sole LandHolder. And soon."

Fear struck Shimokoro to his core.

Wasn't this what he'd wanted all along? To live long enough to see Darikuto and the House of Pearl in its proper place?

Yes. But not at the cost of the LandHolder's soul.

Shimokoro shuddered as he turned his back on the most baleful place he'd ever known.

For the first time he knew doubt.

Yes, The Plan must go on.

But possibly not as Darikuto now had in mind…

Cast List

House of Crystal
Nyati—Capitol
Ibitsima—LandHolder
Haptomi—Head Priest of the Temple of Truth
Akalina—Related to the LandHolder
CrsytalHolders—leaders of House of Crystal warriors

House of Cobalt
Jinyi—Capitol
Kinaki—LandHolder
Belam—Original head priest of the Temple of Truth
Sunli—Current head priest of the Temple of Truth
CollierHolders—leaders of House of Cobalt warriors

House of Gold
Haravik—Capitol
Unnir—LandHolder
Torja—Head Priestess of the Temple of Truth
Emil & Vide—Cousins of Unnir, children of Yudur, the former LandHolder

VeinHolders—leaders of House of Gold warriors

House of Pearl

Yawatan—Capitol
Darikuto—LandHolder
Shimokoro—Head of the Temple of Truth
Benitoyo—Merchant and spy
Chuyoko—head of the warriors
PearlHolders—leaders of House of Pearl warriors

Read More!

Be sure to pick up all the books in the Houses of the Dead trilogy!

Houses Divided
Houses Fallen
Houses Reborn

Available at your favorite retailers!

About the Author

Leah Cutter writes page-turning fiction in exotic locations, such as a magical New Orleans, the ancient Orient, Hungary, the Oregon coast, rural Kentucky, Seattle, Minneapolis, and many others.

She writes literary, fantasy, mystery, science fiction, and horror fiction. Her short fiction has been published in magazines like *Alfred Hitchcock's Mystery Magazine* and *Talebones*, anthologies like Fiction River, and on the web. Her long fiction has been published both by New York publishers as well as small presses.

Find Leah's books on Knotted Road Press at (www.KnottedRoadPress.com)

Follow her blog at www.LeahCutter.com.

Reviews

It's true. Reviews help me sell more books. If you've enjoyed this story, please consider leaving a review of it on your favorite site.

Come someplace new...
Are you a traveler? Do you enjoy exploring strange new worlds, new cultures, new people?

Journey into the various lands envisioned by Leah Cutter.

Sign up for my newsletter and I'll start you on your travels with a free copy of my book, *The Island Sampler*.

I will never spam you or use your email for nefarious purposes. You can also unsubscribe at any time.

http://www.LeahCutter.com/newsletter/

About Knotted Road Press

Knotted Road Press fiction specializes in dynamic writing set in mysterious, exotic locations.

Knotted Road Press non-fiction publishes autobiographies, business books, cookbooks, and how-to books with unique voices.

Knotted Road Press creates DRM-free ebooks as well as high-quality print books for readers around the world.

With authors in a variety of genres including literary, poetry, mystery, fantasy, and science fiction, Knotted Road Press has something for everyone.

Knotted Road Press
www.KnottedRoadPress.com